COLTER SONS BOOK 2

THE ROAMING ADVENTURER

Karen Baney

desert life
media

The Roaming Adventurer: Colter Sons Book 2
By Karen Baney

Unless otherwise indicated, all Scripture quotations are from The ESV® Bible (The Holy Bible, English Standard Version®), copyright © 2001 by Crossway, a publishing ministry of Good News Publishers. Used by permission. All rights reserved.

Publisher:
Desert Life Media, LLC
Gilbert, AZ 85295

www.karenbaney.com

Printed in the United States of America

ISBN-979-8-9858202-9-4

This is a work of fiction. Names, characters, businesses, places, events, and incidents are either the products of the author's imagination or used in a fictitious manner. Any resemblance to actual persons, living or dead, or actual events is purely coincidental.

Put on then, as God's chosen ones, holy and beloved, compassionate hearts, kindness, humility, meekness, and patience, bearing with one another and, if one has a complaint against another, forgiving each other; as the Lord has forgiven you, so you also must forgive. And above all these put on love, which binds everything together in perfect harmony.

—Colossians 3:12-14

CHAPTER I

I could tell you my name, but growing up at my house, I thought it was almost a curse word.

If Mama said my name, Boone, with her hands raised in the air and let them fall to her side, I knew I pressed her to the point of frustration that day.

If Mama said "Boone" with a low growl like a snarling dog going after a jackrabbit for its supper, the next words outta her mouth were something like: wait until my father gets home. It was an odd thing to say. We lived on a ranch, and he was always within earshot of a rifle.

If Mama said my name and wrung her hands at the same time as her eyebrows scrunched together, she just witnessed me do something highly risky that probably caused her heart to lodge up in her throat. Like the time I jumped outta the hay loft hanging onto a rope that wasn't properly secured to anything. I should have busted up something. I had more lives than a cat.

Heaven forbid if Papa said my name. That usually meant I crossed a line that he didn't like. When that happened, I looked into his steely brown eyes, and I knew I had two choices: shut my mouth or get ready to fight. I probably could have bested him; I was not interested in finding out.

Deep down, I knew my mama loved me. Sam was her

favorite. Always has been and always will be, especially after he picked the most perfect woman in the world. Sometimes, I wondered if I was jealous of my irreproachable brother and the bond he had with Mama. It was probably why I did the craziest things to get her attention.

I was the middle Colter son. The devilish handsome red-head that was the spitting image of Mama but in male form. It irritated her I knew I was that good looking. Though, she wished I showed some humility.

Once, I overheard her telling Aunt Julia that I was like Esau in the Bible. I came out all hairy and a half-grown man. To be sure, I started shaving before my older two brothers and muscles just appeared one day when I was six-teen. People thought I was older than James or Sam when they looked at my physique. If they witnessed one of my stunts, then they thought I must be the baby of the family because of my recklessness.

Anyway, Mama still wanted me to settle down and show some humility. She hoped I found a woman that could tame me. I was not the type to be bridled by a living soul. I was just not wired that way. Never have been. Never will be.

Or at least that's what I thought until the year that I met Jack Bennett. That year changed my life in ways that no one, not even Mama, with all her wisdom, could have ever predicted.

CHAPTER 2

Colter Ranch, Arizona Territory
October 5, 1890

BOONE

I woke before sunrise on Sunday morning and saddled Outlaw, my black stallion. He and I understood each other. We were both wild and fearless. Mama called us heedless. She didn't understand the insatiable drive to press myself to the limit.

Once I saddled Outlaw, I mounted him. As soon as dawn colored the sky blue-gray, I kicked him into a full gallop toward the mountain that stood guard over the ranch.

Before the sun crested over the horizon, we arrived at my favorite rocky climb. I tied Outlaw to a post I brought out there years before. Then I stood in front of the rock face and studied it even though I climbed up it more times than I could remember. I chose the most difficult option to stretch and challenge my muscles.

"You run on home if I fall, you hear me?" I asked Outlaw.

He snorted. He would be no help at all.

Then I found my first handhold, followed by my foothold. I pulled my large, muscled frame up to the next hold. My muscles burned as I repeated the process over and over until I reached the top of the rock. Once there, I slung my arm up on the flat surface and pulled my body weight up. Then I turned and sat with my feet dangling over the edge.

Blood pumped through my body, and I breathed hard. My mind focused on and observed details of my surroundings. My soul enjoyed feeling so alive as I watched the sun splay streaks of orange and pink across the sky.

Nothing obstructed my view as I stood on the top of the rock and spread my arms wide. Miles of earth lay before me in every direction. Then I whooped so loud that it echoed across the expanse before I took a deep breath and let it out slowly.

Most folks worship God by standing in a stuffy church singing songs from memory and barely let the words infiltrate their soul. I worshiped God by appreciating the vastness of His creation or watching the sun rise on a cool October morning. I worshiped Him by pushing my body to the limit as lifeblood flowed through my veins.

I sat down on the edge of the rock face and climbed down slowly. After several minutes, my feet rested on solid ground. I waited for my breathing to normalize, then I mounted Outlaw, and he galloped back to the ranch.

Judging by the position of the sun in the sky, I arrived on time for breakfast, so I looped Outlaw's reins over the porch rail. Then I swung the door of the house open.

"It is a fine morning, family!" I declared loudly, startling Mama as she cooked breakfast.

"Boone." She frowned. "Go wash up."

One day I would wash up before she told me to. Then

she would not know how to greet me.

I grabbed a bucket and went outside to the pump and filled it. The cold water stung my skin as I splashed it on my face. I used my shirt to dry it before I refilled the bucket and carried it into the house. Being a thoughtful son, I filled the water reservoir on the stove so it would heat before Mama washed the dishes.

Occasionally, I surprised Mama with such niceties. I received a mumbled "thanks" for my efforts. If I was born two years earlier and named Sam, she would have appreciated it more. I shrugged off the thought, refusing to let it dampen the energy I gained from my early morning climb.

"Preston, I didn't hear you come in last night," Mama said as she set breakfast on the table.

Preston, my youngest brother, groaned. "Me and the boys arrived home around midnight."

I snorted. He woke me up at two in the morning with his stumbling. But if he felt comfortable lying to Mama, who was I to say otherwise?

"Sorry we're late," Ellie Mae, my sister-in-law, said as she entered the house with baby Brody in her arms. My older brother, Sam, carried his other son, Sterling, as he followed behind her.

Ellie Mae set Brody in the highchair between her and Sam, who sat at the foot of the table. Her two-year-old son Sterling squirmed, and Violet took him from Sam.

"Sterling wouldn't settle last night, and Brody woke so many times," Ellie Mae said. "One of those times I heard the ruckus from you, Preston, and the cowboys. Two in the morning is a bit late, don't you think?"

I smiled. It was a callous thought, but I took pleasure when Preston's lies were exposed.

"You smell like a brewery," Grady Thatcher said. He

was Ellie Mae's younger brother.

Preston frowned and took his seat without confirming or denying the accusations.

No meal at our house went smoothly or quietly. Besides Sam, the second oldest of us Colter boys, there was me, then Deacon, and Preston. Since his parents passed on, Grady lived with us. By then, he was like another brother. He was a few years younger than Preston, but older than our baby sister, Violet, and he was best friends with Deacon.

The family had only one girl, Violet, whom we called Vi. She was twelve, a solid ten years younger than me. She was Papa's favorite and Mama's second favorite, after Sam, of course.

"You'll never catch a young woman smelling like that," Vi said.

"Ain't looking for a woman," Preston said.

He wasn't the only one. So far, only Sam had married. James might be a bachelor for life. Me, I had no plans to marry. My job as a surveyor kept me away from home for weeks or months on end. I figured Deacon or Grady would be the next to wed. Preston appeared a long way from wrapping up his rebellious years.

Mama sighed and bowed her head as she waited for Papa to say the blessing. It was the only minute of silence at any meal.

As soon as Papa finished, the chaos resumed. Brody cried, so Ellie Mae excused herself to feed the six-week-old. Sterling failed to adjust to the lost attention, so he squawked at Sam in toddler language. I did not understand him. Somehow, Sam deciphered it and held up a piece of toast.

My life perplexed me. Sometimes I loved the noise and contributed to it more often than not. Yet, days like that day, it bothered me. I returned the previous evening from a two-month job with my employer, Mike Fremont, down in the Bradshaw Mountains, surveying for a mine. A Colter meal was completely opposite of the peace I experienced storytelling around the campfire at night and working in God's creation during the day.

"James is coming for supper," Mama announced. She looked at me. "Said he wants to talk to you about something important."

———

I completely forgot that James would be at Sunday supper. It wasn't until he entered the house for the meal that I remembered.

As soon as Papa blessed the midafternoon meal, James jumped in with his sales pitch. He always schemed some new opportunity.

"Boone, I need your help surveying Hell Canyon."

I frowned. "The Central Arizona Railway already has a line north of here. Isn't Hell Canyon out of the way?"

"It's not for CAR. I'm working on a new project with Frank Murphy."

He glanced at Ellie Mae. Despite being the mother of two young children, she still wrote articles for the Prescott Gazette.

"Mike has said nothing about it," I said as I bit into Mama's delicious melt-in-your-mouth roast. She was the finest cook in the county.

"Your boss won't touch it. Says there's a conflict of interest with the work you are already doing."

The work we did for the mine wasn't a conflict. If he meant a conflict with the railway, it would be for James, too.

"I'd like you to start up your own surveying company. I'll front you the capital if Papa and Sam won't."

"Is this for another railway?" Papa asked as he scowled at James.

Sam sat up straighter.

"Yes. Ellie Mae, you can't print a word of this."

She nodded.

"Aren't you still a vice president at the Central Arizona Railway?" Sam asked.

"For now. This is for a different project."

"Sounds a little unethical," Papa said as he held James's gaze.

James frowned. "It is just a matter of time before Bullock runs CAR into the ground. Prescott will need a new railway."

Sam snorted. "I suppose you and Murphy want to provide it. Tell me, is it going to run through our grazing land?"

James dodged the question. "Boone, will you do it?"

I considered his words. I agreed with Papa that James's actions sounded a little unethical. However, if he had the capital to help me set up my business and he wanted to be my first customer, I jumped at the chance.

"I'll do it. What's your timeline?"

James said he needed the survey report by the end of the year.

"I can't believe you," Sam said as he glared at me. "You know, it's just a matter of time before James runs a railroad through our land."

"Whoa! I'm just conducting a survey of Hell Canyon and other northern parts of the prospective line. I don't want it to go through Colter land."

That was not exactly true. Sam and Papa were pretty adamant about no lines through their land. I was a little more noncommittal.

After the meal, Sam and his brood returned to his house across the yard. James and I strategized in the parlor. He suggested I write to the Surveyor General of the Arizona Territory and his counterpart in California to request their recommendations for an assistant surveyor and crew. So, I spent the afternoon writing the letters and drafting an advertisement to place in newspapers in Tucson, Sacramento, and San Francisco.

The next day, I located the office space, which James front-ed the cost. Then I paid for supplies out of my savings. I agreed to one last job for Mike Fremont that finished before I would interview candidates the first week of November. That also bought me time for my new Gurley Single Vernier Transit to arrive. It was the same model I used surveying with Mike.

I looked forward to running my business and building something great.

CHAPTER 3

Sacramento, California
October 31, 1890

JACLYN

I entered my papa's office. Silas Bennett was the Surveyor General of the State of California. He worked there since I was twelve years old. While I waited for him to return, I sat at his desk and looked over some papers. Was it nosy? Yes. But I learned so much about the business side of surveying from it. So, I did not feel guilty.

A letter from the Arizona Territory caught my eye. I un-folded the letter from Boone Colter. He wrote to my papa to see if he recommended anyone for an assistant surveyor. My heart pounded as I continued to read that Mr. Colter started a new surveying company to support the fledgling railroad companies in Prescott, Arizona, the former capital of the territory.

When I read the job description for the assistant surveyor, I took a deep breath. I could do that job easily. After all, I studied under the Surveyor General of the State of California for six years. I helped Papa make some maps for the state, and I traveled with him and his crew. Most of the men in his crew called me Jack, short for my name, Jaclyn. They thought of me as one of their own.

Every time I traveled with Papa, I pulled my weight. We hunted for game for supper, including me. Even though it was hard, I held the steel measuring tape tight while making sure the plumb bob remained in position and the line remained level. That was critical for accurate measurements. As his assistant surveyor, I assembled, operated, and read the settings on the transit more often than Papa.

So, yes, I knew the job. There was only one significant obstacle. I was a woman. While my papa and his crew accepted a female co-worker, I doubted that any other crew would.

Regardless, I took a fresh sheet of paper from my father's desk and copied down the address and pertinent details. Then I stuffed the paper in my reticule as my father opened the door.

"Good afternoon, Papa," I greeted him.

"Jaclyn, so glad you came by. Are you ready for supper?"

After kissing him on the cheek, I took his offered arm.

We walked a few blocks to Papa's favorite restaurant. Once seated, he smiled at me.

As I sipped iced tea, Papa launched into a conversation I never expected.

"Jaclyn, sweetheart, it's time we discussed your future. You are twenty years old and its past time for you to consider marriage."

I frowned. The last thing I wanted to consider was marriage. "Papa, I don't want to marry and be stuck in the house all the time."

He laughed. "It's not all bad. Your mother, God rest her soul, spent time outdoors regularly while managing a household and caring for you."

As I narrowed my eyes, I stabbed a piece of chicken on my plate before I chomped down on it with great emphasis.

"Why can't I continue to work with you and your crew?"

Papa looked away. Then he sighed heavily as he turned his attention back to me.

"It really is not proper for me to bring you on our jobs. I never should have. After your mother died, it was easier to bring you with me instead of leaving you with a stranger."

"I certainly don't regret it. I've learned so much and I love my job," I said as I hoped he would reconsider.

"When you turned sixteen, it occurred to me it was likely a mistake. As you grew into a lovely woman, I saw the way the crew looked at you."

As I grew more uncomfortable with the conversation, I pushed food around on my plate.

"Then I kept putting off this discussion."

I wished he would have never started it.

"The women your age at church are married with little ones by now. You really ought to marry. Start a family. Give me some grandchildren."

"Please don't make me do this. I love surveying. I would be miserable being a wife and mother."

His lips turned down and his eyes darted away.

"I'm sorry, but I think it is for the best that you give it up and pursue normal womanly activities."

My heart tightened, and my lungs constricted. The traditional role for women held little appeal for me. I was my father's daughter in most ways. Save for one. I was not male. If I was, the conversation would be entirely different.

"I am leaving tomorrow for a three-week trip to oversee the surveying of some state land."

Perhaps he would delay his plans for me a little longer. As my hope grew, I straightened and smiled.

"You will not be joining me."

My smile disappeared as I politely set my silverware down and pushed my plate away, no longer hungry.

"While I am gone, I want you to prepare for your new life. You should have some fashionable dresses made for social dances and other outings. When I return, I will introduce you to some quality, Christian, young men. I expect you to give this your best effort."

I frowned and crossed my arms over my chest.

"I don't expect you to fall in love with the first man that comes along. Please try. Get to know them. Consider courtship. Allow yourself to fall in love."

The server came and took Papa's payment for the meal, giving me the distraction I needed to stand. I wanted to run from the restaurant. To flee far away and never return.

Maybe not never as I would miss Papa.

Instead, I took his arm as he accompanied me home. All the while my mind churned over his announcement.

Once we arrived home, I sought the solace of my room. I opened my reticule and pulled out my notes about the assistant surveyor job in Prescott. That job was what I wanted more than anything. If only I had been born a man.

My mother's words a few months before she passed came to my mind. When I was fourteen years old, I voiced a similar lament to her. Mama said if God wanted me to be a man, I would be. She told me I should be thankful for who He made me to be.

Mostly, I was thankful to be a woman. It was not like I hated it. What I disliked was that the same opportunities for a career were not available to me solely because of my gender.

Slowly, an idea took shape in my mind. What if I could reasonably disguise myself as a young man?

I stood in front of my full-length mirror and studied my body. My bustline was a fair size. Not small, but not large either. I took off my dress and layers of petticoats, leaving only my underwear. Then I pressed my chest flatter with my hands. If I wrapped my chest tight enough, I might minimize it.

My raven black hair trailed down my back to my waist. I never had thick hair like some girls. Mine was thin and fine. It looked nice enough piled on top of my head for a special occasion. Typically, I wore a braid or a tight knot at the base of my neck. If I cut off a few inches, I could keep a feminine length, yet be able to hide it easily under a wig or hat. I schemed into the night planning my disguise.

The next morning, I made breakfast for Papa before he left on his trip. Once he was gone, I pulled a few things from his closet to get an idea of what I needed to purchase. I cut some strips of fabric from an old bed sheet. Then I wrapped my chest as tight as I could. I donned one of Papa's work shirts before I turned to the side. No one would know I was a woman.

Even though Papa's trousers hid my womanly hips, they hung loosely on my body, so I cinched the waistline with a leather belt before I rolled up the pant legs. I put on my work boots that I wore when I surveyed with Papa. There was nothing remotely feminine about those boots.

Then I wound my hair and placed my Panama straw hat on. The ribbon on the hat was too feminine, so I ripped it off as I pondered my reflection in the mirror from my head to my toes.

My smooth skin made me look younger than a man my age. Perhaps a theater supply store would carry a thin adhesive mustache.

I looked at my reflection again. It might work.

After I changed back into a dress, I went shopping for some convincing pieces of clothing. Then I packed only one dress in a trunk along with all my surveying equipment and notebooks. I donned my new disguise and packed a second change of male clothes.

I left a note for Papa propped on the kitchen table, letting him know I traveled to Prescott, Arizona, for a job.

A carriage drove me to the bank where I withdrew enough funds for the trip. Papa paid me a wage similar to the rest of his crew, so I saved a fair amount of money. The carriage delivered me to the train station where I purchased a ticket to Seligman, Arizona. The train station manager said I would have to purchase the ticket from Seligman to Prescott once I arrived there. Within hours, I was on my way.

The trip took two days from Sacramento to Seligman. When I arrived, I stayed the night in a hotel before continuing to Prescott the next day. Once there, I secured a private room at a boardinghouse. The interviews started the next day, so I practiced lowering my voice and planned what I would say in the interview.

Then I prayed, something I should have done before I started my journey. I prayed that Mr. Colter would find my skills satisfactory and not discover my true identity.

CHAPTER 4

Prescott, Arizona Territory
November 5, 1890

BOONE

When I arrived in town, a line of men trailed down the better part of the block near my office. That was more interest than I expected. Men of all sizes and shapes stood in the line. I rode past them and took Outlaw to the livery before I grabbed my satchel and saddlebags.

As I walked toward the front door of my office, I studied the men. Based on looks alone, I almost ruled out the plump or haggard men. Instead, I decided to interview them all until I found an assistant surveyor and three men for the crew. I thought they might surprise me and be ready for the tough physical challenges of the job.

When I opened the door for the first man, he tripped over the threshold. He was a beefy fellow but unsteady on his feet. Once I pictured him stumbling and falling over the edge of a cliff in my mind's eye, I thanked him for his time and sent him on his way.

After an hour, a strange looking fellow approached. He

had dark hair. He was short and somewhat thin, though he appeared to be a sturdy young man.

"Jack Bennett," he introduced himself. He held out his hand for a firm handshake while he met my gaze. His hands seemed a little soft.

When my eyes connected with his, I stared. I couldn't help it. His left eye was amber, and his right eye was green, something I'd never seen before. Didn't think it was possible.

Shaking off the unsettling feeling, I forced myself to pay attention to what he said as I motioned for him to sit in a chair across from my desk. Then I took a seat.

"I worked with the Surveyor General of the State of California for the past six years."

As he listed off an extensive set of qualifications, I studied him. His clothes hung loosely on his thin frame. His posture remained ramrod straight and his dark hair peeked out from under his straw hat. Many surveyors favored such a hat. His thin mustache barely went the length of his upper lip. He impressed me as a man who hadn't quite hit his last growth spurt.

"How old are you?" I asked.

"Twenty."

Older than he appeared. I frowned. "I thought you said you worked with the Surveyor General for six years."

He cleared his throat. "I started when I was fourteen. I lied to him about my age at the time as I needed the job. When I proved my value, he kept me on."

I narrowed my eyes. Something seemed off about the young man. Unable to put my finger on it, I continued the interview.

"What type of transit did you use?"

"We used a single vernier transit. 1856 Gurley model.

My boss refused to upgrade to one of the newer models, though I used the 1874 Gurley on a recent trip. It has some nice new features. I particularly like the smoother mechanics of the siting telescope."

My 1874 Gurley Single Vernier Transit arrived the day before, though I did not unpack it at that point.

I asked Jack a few more questions specifically about how to read the angles from the instrument, what methods his previous crew used to plumb the steel tape line, and how they worked to clear the line.

Towards the end of the interview, I asked him to solve a math problem similar to one we would encounter in the field. I offered Jack a slide rule calculator, pencil, and piece of paper to solve the problem. He jotted down some values as I described the imaginary readings I took from the transit. Then within seconds, he solved the problem without writing out the math on the paper or touching the calculator.

"How do you do that?" I asked. "With no help."

He shrugged. "Math is easy for me, and I see the answer in my mind. Typically, I record the measurements, write the answer, and then I double check it back in the office when we return to town. I have yet to be wrong."

Clearly an experienced surveyor; I liked his cautious approach. Every surveyor and assistant learned early on the value of accurate records in the field. Inaccurate records could require repeating the survey, a cost no employer desired, including me.

I wondered why Jack applied for the assistant position when he obviously held the skills to run his own crew. After an hour interview, Jack proved to be the most qualified candidate so I offered him the job.

"We start tomorrow," I said. "I expect everyone in camp to contribute to camp life. Hunting, cleaning, cooking."

"Not a problem," he said as he shook my hand.

"We'll leave shortly after dawn once everything is packed."

"Thank you, Mr. Colter."

I snorted. "That's my father's name. Just call me Boone."

"Alright. Boone it is."

Throughout the afternoon, I interviewed and hired three more men for the crew. One of them, Holt Greenvale, worked with me on one trip with Mike. Holt understood geology and mineralogy better than most. He brought a friend, Charlie Ransom, that he worked with on some other crews. Charlie was an expert botanist, and his identification of plant life rivaled my own. Then I hired a young man named Dustin Boyd. He looked strong and would be an asset when loading and unloading our gear as well as carrying the heaviest equipment to remote areas. He seemed rather green, but he had good references and a great attitude. I could teach him anything else he needed to know.

After I finished the interviews, I unpacked the transit. I set it up and practiced using it. Then I placed it back into its case. I packed other provisions and supplies into smaller crates and packs that would fit on a mule's back. Then I rented a wagon and hauled the goods over to the train station where I paid the fee to store the goods overnight.

By the time I returned to my office, James waited for me there.

"You all set?" he asked.

"Yes. Got a good crew. We'll head out in the morning."

"Confidentiality is important. Make certain your crew does not speak to anyone about it. Also, when you're in Ash Fork, be aware of who is listening."

I assured him all would be well. Sometimes James needed to control everything. We were professionals and would keep our client's business to ourselves.

CHAPTER 5

JACLYN

I could not believe Boone Colter offered me the job. As I repacked my trunk with the things I did not need for the trip, I offered a prayer of gratitude to God. The boardinghouse owner kindly offered to store my trunk until I returned which saved me the expense of renting a room while I traipsed across the Arizona wilderness. I packed everything else in my saddlebags. Thankfully, Boone provided most of the equipment. Still, I preferred to use my notebook, pencils, and drafting compass.

Before dawn cast brilliant colors across the sky, I arrived at Colter Surveying, and I knocked on the door.

A groggy, shirtless Boone opened it. My heart skittered at the sight of his undershirt which revealed well-defined muscular arms. His bright red hair stood at all angles contrasting nicely with his brilliant blue eyes. A full red beard covered his chin, hiding his mouth.

"Jack. Come on in."

I coughed to chase away the strange feelings.

"Morning."

My eyes remained glued to his back while he donned a white cotton shirt and snapped his suspenders in place. My breath left me. While working for my papa, I'd seen dozens of half-dressed men. My reaction to Boone confused me.

"Care for some coffee," he said as he held up the pot.

"Sure." I squeaked.

His large, thick, calloused fingers brushed mine as I took the cup from his hands. A scar ran across his right hand from his second knuckle toward his thumb. He noticed me staring at it.

"Fishing accident as a kid." His grin revealed his perfect teeth as his eyes lit up. "I won, and he lost. Tasty fellow."

I hid my smile behind my coffee cup.

After he combed his hair and beard, he slapped a cowboy hat on his head. I wondered if it ever grew too hot. That was why I preferred my straw hat.

A few minutes later, three men joined us.

"Jack Bennett," I introduced myself, keeping my voice low. I gave each man a firm handshake.

Dustin Boyd reminded me a bit of the Sicilian on Papa's crew, with his dark brown eyes and dark brown hair. Even though he was the youngest, he looked strong and sturdy.

Holt Greenvale stood as tall as Boone, nearly a foot taller than me. For a moment, I worried that my height might give me away. When Holt slapped me on the back, like men did, I released my fear. A wad of tobacco bulged his lower lip, and his dark brown eyes were friendly.

The last member of the crew was Charlie Ransom. I held back a snicker at his name. Ransom. I certainly hoped there would be no kidnappings or ransoms on our journey.

"I already have most of our gear packed and waiting at the train station," Boone said. "We'll take the train up to Seligman, then over to Ash Fork. Once we're in Ash Fork, we'll stay the night. Since we've got horses, we'll camp outside of town. Already have a suitable spot in mind. Then tomorrow we'll start mapping the route to Hell Canyon."

"Hell Canyon!" Holt hollered and shook his head. "That's dangerous."

"I know," Boone said with a grin. "It's gonna be fun."

Charlie quirked an eyebrow. Dustin and I didn't react. I gathered we were in for a surprise.

Boone led the way to the livery to pick up his spirited black stallion. Holt and Charlie retrieved their horses. Boone rented two horses, one for me and one for Dustin. My sable-colored mare looked about as energetic as a rock. Dustin's dappled gelding at least appeared to have a heartbeat.

We led the horses to the train station and handed them to a porter who loaded them on a car. Then we gave the last of our things to the baggage car attendant before we boarded the train and took our seats.

I sat in a window seat. When Boone slid into the seat next to me, I felt tiny, as his broad shoulders spanned the width of the seat causing his arm to encroach into my space. I scooted closer to the window so I would not touch him.

Across the aisle, Holt and Charlie sat together. Dustin sat in front of them in the aisle seat.

When the train pulled away, Boone started the conversation.

"Holt, you remember that job we did for Mike?"

Holt nodded.

"And the boulder hopping?"

"If I recall, you were the only one who hopped any boulders. The rest of us took the safer, mule-friendly route."

Boone laughed. It was a hearty sound that bubbled up from his belly. He slapped a hand on his leg. "It was so much fun. I really enjoyed scaling that boulder."

"How big was it?" Dustin asked.

"Probably about forty feet tall."

Dustin's jaw dropped.

"Forty feet?" Charlie asked. "That's insane."

As I shifted in my seat, I swallowed hard. Seemed Boone's tolerance for risk did not align with mine.

Boone leaned forward. "Nearly lost a fingernail on that one. Scraped it half off when my hand slipped. I recovered. It grew back. No big deal."

"How high were you when it happened?" I asked as my stomach clenched.

He shrugged. "About twenty-five feet."

I blinked. A twenty-five-foot drop would do some damage to a body. Boone seemed entirely unconcerned.

"Do you regularly climb over forty-foot boulders?" I asked under my breath.

My face warmed as he turned to face me. No problem with his hearing.

"No. I regularly scale the side of a cliff near my home to hone my skills."

I shook my head.

"Come on, Jack. Don't tell me you are afraid of heights?"

"Afraid of heights?" I snorted. "No. Afraid of stupidity? Yes. I prefer working with men who won't get me killed since I hope to settle down and have a family someday." That last part was not true, but it sounded like something a man might say.

He rolled his eyes. "It's not stupidity when a man knows the capabilities and limits of his own body. God gave me these muscles." He flexed his biceps and wiggled his eyebrows as a grin stretched across his face. "I have no problem putting them to good use."

I grunted before I turned to gaze out the window. He regaled the crew with stories of other ill-advised adventures.

The landscape changed from forest to large rocks and boulders as big or bigger than the one Boone described. The train twisted and winded along the valley floor and through several large washes. I read about Arizona's monsoons on the train ride to the territory. The massive rainstorms flared up with little notice and could dump large volumes of water in seconds which caused flash floods.

Several considerations ran around in my head for the surveying trip. Though I found the curves in the train ride moderately annoying, I figured they skipped building bridges in some areas because of the cost. Laying tracks in a wash bed was significantly less costly than shipping in steel trusses for the bridge.

"Who is sponsoring this trip?" I asked Boone.

"Shh." He lowered his voice to a whisper. "A competing railroad for a shorter connector route from Prescott to the A&P. Keep quiet about it."

"Of course. When I know about the customer, I can anticipate the additional information they'll expect. I'm sure a railroad wants to know where to flatten out the road with blasting or where bridges might be more cost-effective."

As if he had not expected me to consider such critical things, his eyes widened.

"We need to do that, right?" I asked.

"Of course. I just never worked with someone on my crew who thought about it. It was usually me or Mike that did that."

"Who is Mike?"

"He was my mentor, and I was his assistant."

"So, you are the chief surveyor, and I am your assistant. I am more than equal to the task."

He stroked his long red beard. "You haven't let me down yet."

Yet. I held back a sigh. Even with my disguise, I would have to work twice as hard to prove myself capable of all the aspects of the job.

CHAPTER 6

BOONE

We arrived in Ash Fork before noon, and we retrieved our things from the train station. Then I rented several pack mules for our supplies from the Ash Fork livery. Our journey involved narrow trails, and sometimes, no trails at all. A wagon was useless.

After we secured the supplies to the pack mules, we headed south out of Ash Fork.

"I think a mule would be faster than this blasted mare," Jack complained.

Outlaw snorted at the slow pace. Jack kicked his mare, and it finally found some energy. He rode up next to me on the wide flat trail out of Ash Fork.

"Do we have any maps or are we trail blazin'?" he asked.

"Mostly trail blazing."

"You want me to sketch as we go?"

Again, he surprised me with his foresight. "Probably a good idea. Seems like your mare is slow enough, it'll be easy."

As he retrieved a notebook from his saddlebag, he grunted before he removed one leg from his stirrup and crossed it over the horn of his saddle to provide a level surface for his notebook. He loosely held the reins and notebook with one hand while sketching with the other. Interesting technique. It seemed to work for him.

"How far do you think that mountain range is from here?" I asked.

He glanced up. "Seven point three six miles."

I laughed. "That's pretty precise."

"I'm a precise person."

My guess was around eight to ten miles. I almost wanted to unpack the transit to measure it and prove him wrong. Or right.

Without looking up, he added, "I suppose you were looking for more of a range? Seven to seven and half miles."

He glanced up and smiled. He was teasing.

"Funny."

We rode for several hours with only a few breaks to stretch our legs and rest the horses.

When the sun lowered in the sky, we found an area to camp with plenty of grass for the horses and mules to munch on. Dustin volunteered to find some firewood but came back empty-handed. The area was full of low scrub brush and ironwood trees, so I suggested he cut one or two down and into smaller pieces. They only stood five to ten feet tall.

As Holt cleared away the grass from an area, Charlie looked for several rocks for a fire ring. While Jack continued to work on his map, I retrieved my spyglass and scanned the distance. No sign of natives. Right before the sun dipped below the horizon, Dustin's fire blazed.

"We've got some biscuits and bacon. My mama kindly made them for us," I said.

"I'm starving," Dustin said as he took the offered food.

Everyone else ate heartily except Jack. He nibbled on a biscuit and only ate two pieces of bacon. No wonder he was so small. I slapped him on the shoulder.

"Eat up. You'll need your energy for tomorrow. We need to cover twice as much ground if we're going to make it to Hell Canyon by Monday."

"I'm fine."

When he handed me his map, I held it toward the firelight to get a better look at it. I stood still and raised my eyebrows.

As I slowly shook my head, I said, "That's incredibly detailed."

"I figure if we are measuring on the way back, we can fill in the distances. I penciled in rough estimates."

I handed the notebook back to Jack. As I rubbed a hand over my beard, I sat by the fire. When I was sixteen years old, six years ago, I started working with Mike. Jack worked for his boss for six years as well. Yet, he seemed better than me at cartography and math. His results were more like a man with ten or more years' experience.

For a moment, I felt threatened. I shrugged it off. I knew the job. These men were my employees. It did not matter if Jack was better than me in those areas. I brought plenty to the expedition.

We did not unpack our tents that night but slept under the stars with a blanket near the fire.

The next morning, we broke camp just after dawn and arrived at Hell Canyon in the late afternoon. We set up camp on the northern rim of the canyon. Dustin removed the supplies from the donkeys before he set up a temporary corral for the mules and horses. Holt searched for firewood. Charlie dug a fire pit and set up his tent while I set up mine. Jack worked on his map. When he finished, he set up his tent. Then he left to scout the area. He returned just before dusk.

"Anything of interest?" I asked.

"I think one of us should hang out down in the canyon in that area tomorrow. I saw some mule deer. Might make a nice supper for a few days."

"We'll see how Dustin is with a rifle," I said.

"I also think we should head east for the crossing area. It looked like the canyon might be narrower there. Be easier to build a bridge if our client wants to."

"After we find the best crossing for a bridge, I want to survey along the canyon floor. I imagine they will want an alternate route."

Jack agreed before he retired to his tent. The rest of us stay-ed up telling stories for a few hours before we turned in.

The next morning, I unpacked the surveying equip-ment. Jack, Charlie, Holt, and I rode along the rim to the area Jack mentioned. The rocky edge of the canyon sloped downward at a shallower angle for about twenty-five feet before it dropped deep into the canyon. It was a reasonable spot for a bridge as the shallower slopes on both sides would make a good anchoring point for a bridge.

"How deep do you think it is?" Charlie asked.

"Three hundred feet," Jack answered. Then he smirked. "Give or take ten feet."

I nodded as I figured the same.

"Charlie," I said. "I'm thinking we'll run a line starting around here and head southwest from there. You and Holt study the flora and geology."

That first day, we fleshed out a rough plan for the next few weeks. I smiled as we walked back to camp. While the rest of us cared for the animals, Jack cooked supper. The crew worked well together, and my confidence soared as I took pride in my new team. It felt good to lead such a fine group.

CHAPTER 7

JACLYN

The next morning, we cleared the line. It was important to remove all obstacles from the line of sight in order to get ac-curate readings from the transit. I set up the transit for Boone. Then he held the end of the one-hundred-foot steel tape while he grasped the plumb bob chain tight against it. As the plumb bob's weight dangled over the side of the tape, I crouched down and instructed him to make minor adjustments until the chain was perfectly perpendicular to the tape.

"Whatcha thinking, boss? Run the line slightly more west than south?" I asked.

"You see that tree on the rim of the canyon?"

"Yup."

"That's our landmark. We need to clear the line straight that direction."

"Got it."

I spoke with Holt, Charlie, and Dustin. They cleared the brush to make a three-foot wide path while I carried the steel tape. It grew heavier the longer I waited for them.

Eventually, Dustin volunteered to carry the tape for a while. I flexed my fingers and stretched my arms over my head before I accepted the machete from Dustin.

"Make sure you don't let the tape fold back on itself. If that happens, it'll snap in half and need replaced. If we cut the trip short because of a busted tape measure, Boone won't be pleased."

Dustin grunted.

"Jack!"

I turned toward Boone fifty yards behind us. He motioned to my left.

"Line is off course!"

Then I stepped to my left. He motioned me further, and I took another step. He waved me back to my right a half step.

Doggone. We needed to go back ten yards to clear the brush along the corrected line.

"Dustin, you stand here."

As I looked to Boone, he gave a thumbs up.

"Holt, Charlie, we got a course correction."

They followed me back to where the line hovered over some brush. The three of us hacked at limbs and uprooted smaller bushes. The November sun beat down on my back. I longed for a bath and some shade.

Bushwhacking days were my least favorite. The stronger members of the team handled it better than me. I wished I could trade places with my large, well-muscled employer. But I was the assistant, and it was my job to manage the line.

"Jack!"

I stood to my full height and rotated my head to stretch my neck before I looked Boone's way. He motioned me to come to him.

As I walked back to his position, I shook out my arms. Then I propped my elbow in my opposite hand to stretch my shoulder before I stretched the other one.

"Boss?"

"Here, you take this. I need a break and it looks like you could use a change."

Once I took the tape from his fingers, careful to place my thumb over the chain of the plumb bob, he crouched down to confirm the line remained level.

"You're doing good," he said. "I'm guessing clearing the line isn't your favorite thing to do."

I turned my lips up in a half-smile despite the weariness in my body. "Much better at math."

He heartily laughed for a few seconds before he walked down the line to join the others. I watched as he made quick work of the last fifty yards.

By the time we cleared the line, the sun lowered in the sky. Boone marked several spots in the dirt along the line so we could pick up our work the next day.

Then he helped Dustin coil the steel tape so it wouldn't twist or break. When he finally took the tape from my hands, I was ready to collapse as holding the steel tape taut pained me, unlike it did for a larger, muscular man like Boone. Even though it was my least favorite task, I would do it again in order to keep my job.

I flexed my fingers and rubbed the palm of my right hand the entire walk back to camp where I awkwardly fell to the ground in my attempt to sit gracefully. Thankfully, it was not my turn to cook. Holt warmed some beans and coffee over the fire. We skipped lunch as we usually did on a day like that. We were all starved. Most of the men inhaled their food. As I felt a little queasy from expending so much physical energy, I ate slower.

As soon as supper was over, I went into my tent and listened to the sound of Boone's voice regaling the crew with wild stories of past expeditions. I liked the deepness of his voice and the animation in his inflection brought the stories to life. In a few minutes, I passed out.

The next morning, I woke at dawn and hid my hair under my hat, so I looked like a man. I repositioned my mustache before I exited my tent. My disguise held up well.

I walked from camp to find a place to relieve myself. Of course, I went further away than the others because I had a secret to keep.

When I returned to camp, I worked out some of the stiffness in my legs and arms. Or so I thought until I reached down for the coffeepot. I whimpered.

"Sore?"

I closed my eyes at the sound of Boone's voice behind me.

"Be fine when we move around again."

He snorted, and I got the feeling he was not convinced.

I opened our water barrel. "We ought to refill this at the river bottom tomorrow."

"I'll send Dustin. We should be fine without him this morning since the line is clear. Holt and Charlie can hold the line while you help me with the readings."

The other three men exited their tents. Each stretched and groaned as they started moving. Guess I wasn't the only one sore.

"Coffee?" I asked as I poured them each a cup.

"Bless you, Jack," Dustin said.

Holt and Charlie grunted in approval. I hid a smile.

After a week, I knew each of their quirks. Dustin was by far the politest young man I ever worked with. He often verbalized his gratitude for the opportunity and soaked up every bit of knowledge any of us shared. Wild and animated described the essence of Boone. Yet, he worked with a singular focus which reminded me of my papa.

A tug on my heart turned my thoughts to home. When Papa returned from his trip, he would be hurt and angry that I left. I brushed the guilt aside as I handed out some biscuits and bacon. I did not know how Boone's mama made biscuits that stayed soft for a week, but I owed the woman a debt of gratitude.

Then there was Holt. His surly demeanor usually cleared up after his second cup of coffee. His eyes continually studied the ground and dirt. I suppose it made sense given his interest in geology and mineralogy. Charlie usually woke up after the first half of his coffee. He often drew pictures of the plant life in the morning. His memory was excellent.

Once breakfast was over, Dustin lagged to care for the animals and refill the water barrels. The rest of us headed to the site.

Boone carried the steel tape, a job usually delegated to the assistant. My relief may not have been clear, but I felt it all the same. My notebook was significantly lighter than the steel tape.

When we arrived, he held the end of the line as I helped him settle the plumb bob in place. Then Holt began unrolling the steel tape. He manned the center of the line and Charlie took up the far end. After I checked each of their plumb bobs, making sure the line was level, I jogged back down to help Boone.

Boone sited the landmark tree with the transit. Then he read off several angles from the vernier on the transit as I jotted the numbers down. He finished by reading off the compass settings which I diligently recorded.

While I sat on the ground with my legs crossed, I balanced my notebook in my lap. Then I computed several calculations. Boone read off a few more numbers. Then he let the line slack and signaled Charlie and Holt to bring it in.

Within minutes, I completed my calculations. I drew a map and noted important distances. Charlie stood over me and pointed out the important plants to mark. Holt rattled off soil conditions and minerals found in the samples he took near the edge of the cliff.

At last, I handed the notebook and pencil to Boone to double check my math.

He chuckled. "Not a single mistake."

When he held out his hand to help me up, tingles traveled up my arm. My breath caught as my eyes connected with his and I saw admiration. I looked away quickly lest I reveal my secret with a single gaze. Then I brushed the dirt from my pants.

"Another job well done, boys," Boone said.

Even though it was early in the afternoon, we accomplished our goal for the day, so Boone suggested we hike down to the river bottom. We dumped our gear at camp before Dustin joined us. Then we walked the path to the river. My throat constricted the closer we came. I couldn't swim with the guys even if I desperately wanted a bath.

When we reached the river bottom, to my utter dismay, Boone stripped down as he ran into the water hooting all the way. I noticed too much detail about his back before I averted my eyes. I swallowed hard.

The other men undressed in a civilized manner, but I hurried further upstream.

"Jack! Come on in!" Boone hollered after me.

When my face flushed, I waved a hand behind me, and I walked for another fifteen minutes upstream, praying none of them followed me. Once I found a bend in the river that offered some privacy, I undressed, unpinned my hair, and unraveled the binding over my chest before I waded into the river.

The cold water felt soothing after days of hard work. I scrubbed my hair then twisted out as much water as I could. After I pinned it up, I stepped from the river. Then I bound my chest and dressed. I just put my hat on when I heard a noise behind me. I turned to look as I snagged my boots and socks from the riverbank.

"Why'd you run off?" Boone asked.

As I pulled on my socks, I sat on a rock. I lowered my voice and added a tinge of gruffness. "I'm a private person, Boone. Don't care for the ruckus when I bathe."

He frowned and his gaze traveled from my head to my toes as I tied the laces on my boots. Then he let out a sigh.

"See any fish?"

I grunted. "Don't think fish frequent this river."

I stood and adjusted my hat. As he continued to study me, my throat constricted. I figured he suspected something.

When he said nothing more, I released a long breath. I picked up the rifle I brought with me.

"I'll scrounge around for a deer or quail or something. You go back up to camp."

He swiped my rifle from my hands and narrowed his eyes. When I tried to take my rifle back, he held it above his head.

"What's the deal with you, Jack?"

"Give it back."

He studied me for another minute. Then he finally handed my rifle back and stalked off. Surely, he suspected something. I only hoped he'd never think I was a woman.

CHAPTER 8

BOONE

In all my years of surveying, I never witnessed a crew member leave to swim alone. When Jack did, I almost ran after him. Foolish man. A river bottom was a vulnerable position. A small man like him would be easy pickin' for hostiles.

Hunting was a little different, as we kept to the shadows of the brush to stalk our prey. We weren't out in the open.

When I found Jack, he grabbed his shoes and put on his socks. I confronted him. His answer did nothing to stem my concern. Private person, my foot. I spat as I walked away from him before I said something I regretted. Instead, I ran up the trail. Physical exertion always helped me work through things that bothered my mind.

In my time, I met all kinds of men, but Jack was the most perplexing of all. He kept to himself in odd ways, like walking fifteen minutes upstream out of earshot and eyesight of the rest of the crew. Maybe California wasn't as dangerous as Arizona. On several expeditions, I faced Indians, rustlers, and outlaws. We stuck together.

The day I hired Jack, I felt something was off. Perhaps, I

should have trusted my gut more. Still bugged me he had the mental acuity and experience to run his own outfit. Physical stamina was a bit of a concern after the previous day as he barely made it through supper before he collapsed in his tent. Perhaps that was why he didn't run his own outfit. Some crews might not respect a leader that couldn't hold his own.

At last, I reached the rim of the canyon. My heart pounded, and I stood for a few minutes to get my breathing under control. Blood pumped through my veins reminding me how good life was.

When I heard the rapport of the rifle, my eyes scanned the river bottom. Then I saw the mule deer fall. Jack stood over the animal and slit its neck, then began dressing the deer like an expert hunter. I sighed and shook my head. Clearly, he was good at that too.

I watched as he struggled to carry the enormous beast. At first, he dragged it some distance. It would be easier to bring it up the canyon and finish butchering it at camp. He kneeled and tried a few times, unsuccessfully, to lift the animal to his shoulders.

As guilt niggled my gut, I swore under my breath and headed down to help. Once I was in earshot, I called out to him.

"Need some help?" I asked only slightly out of breath.

"Ah. Guess so."

I frowned as I hoisted the animal over my shoulders and carried it like a rag doll up the canyon.

"Never been good at hauling the larger game," he said. "Sorry to disappoint you, boss."

My mama's words tumbled out of my mouth. "We all have our different strengths. Saw your kill shot. You made it look easy."

"That's never been my challenge." Jack laughed. "Guess I owe you one."

"It's all good. Thanks for supper."

After I dumped the carcass down on the ground near camp, Jack and I carved it up.

"Arizona isn't like California," I said. "It's important that we stick together, especially in open areas."

"Is it?" Jack challenged me. "Then why do you let Dustin fetch water by himself? Why don't we hunt in groups?"

I frowned. "Maybe we should."

Jack snorted. "Is this because of my stature?"

"Whoa, hold up." I stopped working on the deer. "The rule applies to us all."

"Ha! It is." Jack cleaned his knife. "I get it. I'm small. You don't think I can pull my weight or fend off a band of outlaws. You know nothing about me, Boone Colter."

He sheathed his knife and picked up the meat.

"We can't all be built like a bear. Some of us are small and stealthy, like a bobcat. I know you hike to the work site before anyone else wakes up to watch the sunrise by your-self. You think no one and nothing can touch you. But even a bear has weaknesses."

Then he stormed toward camp. I sighed and followed behind him. Even though he made a few good points, I didn't want to hear them. Right about then I wished I could get some advice from Mike.

When the crew saw the fresh meat, they shouted for joy.

"We'll feast like kings tonight!" Dustin exclaimed.

Holt slapped Jack on the back as Charlie started cooking. For the first time, Jack stayed with the rest of us after supper.

After I finished recounting one of my adventures, Jack spoke up.

"I got one for ya. On an expedition in the Cascades with my p— boss, I had hunting duty. I spent some time studying the path and came across elk tracks. That time, my boss paired up with me."

He turned his different colored eyes on me and held my gaze.

"We didn't hunt alone. Too dangerous in California."

I cleared my throat and frowned.

"Anyway, I tracked that elk for twenty minutes before I found him. There he stood in a clearing eating on grass completely unaware of me. I glanced over my shoulder and saw my boss a few yards back. I leveled my rifle and took a deep breath."

"Before I got the shot off, I heard a twig snap to my right. My boss was to my left. My head swiveled to my right, and you'll never guess what I saw."

"A snake?" Dustin guessed.

Jack laughed and shook his head. "No."

Under his intense stare, I shifted my position on the ground.

"A bobcat. His steely yellow eyes locked with mine. I held his gaze for several seconds as I slowly repositioned the butt of my rifle toward him."

"He was too close for me to get a clean shot if he lunged. I figured I could at least knock him in the head with the butt if he swiped at me."

"What happened?" Dustin waited for Jack to finish.

"I just stared at that bobcat for another ten seconds. Then he darted off."

I shook my head.

"Best I can figure, my weird eyes scared him. Don't think he saw a man with one amber and one green eye before."

Charlie burst out laughing. Holt chuckled. Still wary of Jack's motives, I smiled.

"Did you get the elk?" Dustin asked.

"Funny you should ask. While I stared down the bobcat, my boss saw the elk and fired a minute after the bobcat skedaddled. We ate well that night."

Jack laughed. "Good thing we got that elk. Our supplies were running low, and we were a group of twenty men. We'd been out for two months and neared the end of the job. That elk fed us for a few days and let us finish without starving."

"Were you mad your boss got the shot?" Dustin asked.

"Not at all. I was glad a bobcat did not maul me."

He looked my direction again and nodded. I understood his silent message. He could handle himself.

As I retired to my tent for the night, I admitted Jack appeared capable of a lot of things. One of the best surveyors I worked with. The job. The camp life. The only thing that bothered him were the more physically demanding days. Still, I couldn't shake the feeling he was hiding something.

CHAPTER 9

JACLYN

Boone didn't bug me again about occasionally ditching the rest of the crew after I told my bobcat story. Good thing too. There was too much work for camp drama.

The last trip I went on with my papa was over six months before I started my job with Boone. I was out of shape when we first arrived. My stamina improved the longer we were in the field. I think Boone noticed and left me alone.

"Ready to scale a cliff?" he asked as he loaded the rope ladder and a few other supplies on the back of a mule.

"Finally going over the side." As my excitement grew, I smiled. I felt strong, and confident I knew how to handle the situation.

He laughed. "Good."

We walked the mule to the work site and unloaded him.

"Watcha think? Can we anchor to this tree?" Boone asked.

Charlie studied it. He pushed on it. No give. "I think it'll do. Looks like it's been here a long time."

"We'll also loop the end of the ropes around that boulder," Holt suggested. "Better to have a secondary anchor just in case. Some of these trees don't grow deep roots."

"Good call," Boone said.

I studied him, convinced that it had been his plan all along. I found it interesting how he let others think it was their idea instead of his.

"You want to go first, Jack?"

"Sure thing, boss."

I put on my special tool belt which held a small notepad, pencil, and site. A few small jars sat in the pouch on my belt for soil and rock samples. I slid a miniature pickax into a loop on my belt. Then I donned my leather gloves and picked up the rope.

The rope ladder was about one hundred feet long. By my estimation, it would only take us about a third of the way down into the canyon. We needed to study the wall of the canyon and bring up some samples for Holt besides measuring the depth as best we could.

The first part of the slope was a mild angle, so I held onto the rope and quickly backed down that section. Once I reached the steep drop off, my heart pounded. Placing the wooden platform for the first section was always the most difficult. The two lengths of rope had several loops every few feet where we placed a board seat, like a boatswain seat. It allowed us to stop and stay at a specific depth for an extended time.

Carefully, I wrapped the rope loosely around my left arm. Then I leaned back and walked down the side of the cliff to the first spot. I used my right hand to slide the board seat into the loop on the right rope and then the left. I secured it with a temporary knot. Then, I tested it.

"Holds me fine!" I yelled up to Boone. "I don't know if it'll hold a bear though."

The sound of his chuckle echoed off the canyon walls. Within a few minutes, he joined me on the board.

"Guess it'll hold a bear and bobcat," he teased.

He studied the face of the canyon wall. "So far it looks like we've got some limestone and basalt. Not bad. Should be a solid place to anchor the first set of trusses. Let's get a measurement."

We both counted the knots on the rope ladder which were strategically placed at consistent intervals of three feet.

"I've got twenty-two feet," I said.

"Agreed." I noted the measurement.

"Ready for the next descent?" he asked.

I nodded.

After he wrapped his right arm on the right rope and found a sure foothold, I pulled the left side of the rope up toward me and wrapped it around my arm. Then I removed the board and started down. The next section curved inward. My heart pounded loudly in my ears until I found a sure foothold. I placed the board, tested it, then Boone joined me. We continued the process without incident for the first sixty feet down the canyon wall.

The next time I wrapped the rope around my left arm, I started down with the board. My foot slipped. Then my other foot flew out from under me. My body smashed hard against the rock face. I slid a few feet before the rope around my arm stopped my fall. The board fell into the canyon below. Blood oozed down my face. My breaths came in short bursts. I tried to gain my footing. There was nothing to stand against. My body weight pulled the rope around my arm taut. Pain seared through my shoulder as I heard a loud snap.

God, please no.

I kicked my feet trying to find some foothold. Nothing.

One kick pushed my body away from the wall. I swung back hitting it full force. As my head cracked against the canyon wall, my hat came off. My hair fell around my shoulders. My breathing shallowed and my eyes failed to focus on anything. The pain overwhelmed me.

Then all went black.

CHAPTER 10

BOONE

My heart raced as I felt the line go slack below me. Then I heard the clatter of the board seat as it dropped to the canyon floor. I looked down.

"Jack!"

As he slammed into the side of the canyon wall, I saw him. I heard the loud snap and prayed his arm wasn't broken. He slipped down several feet before the rope tightened around his arm and stopped his descent. Trails of blood ran down his face.

Then long raven black hair spilled from his hat. My breath caught at the unexpected sight. My mind failed to process the implications.

My brain kicked in and overrode the adrenaline coursing through my veins. He would die if I didn't get down there soon. I loosened the rope on my arm. Then I looped a section of rope around my leg and intentionally slid down the rope with little control until I reached my target. I tightened my hold and looped a section over my right arm once I was level with Jack.

His unconscious body swung from the rope, held in

place by the rope cutting off the circulation in his arm. His face was pale.

I found a good foothold to move closer to him. As soon as I caught him around the waist, so many things made sense.

Jack was not a man.

The long raven black hair tickled my face as I pulled her close. I wrapped the rope around her waist and anchored her against my body, forcing myself to ignore the shock of her secret revealed and how she felt against me. If we were both gonna get out of there alive, I must focus on saving us.

The section of rope around her arm wouldn't budge. I reached for my knife and cut through the rope below her. It slithered to the canyon floor. Then I double checked to make sure we were both secure. When I was certain, I cut the rope above her arm. Her body collided with mine, and she groaned.

"Jack, are you with me?"

"Boone?" Her voice sounded weak.

"Can you hold on to me?"

"Yes."

When she put her arms around my neck, she screamed in pain.

"Just use your good arm. I've got you."

I wasn't sure how to climb back up. The immediate danger passed, so I took a few seconds to think through my options.

"Do you think you can lock your legs around my waist?" I asked. "Hold on tight."

She moaned. "Yes."

The breath left my lungs when she did. Her womanly curves pressed close against me. She hid them well with her loose shirt. I swallowed hard and forced myself to ignore the sensations coursing through my body. Leaning back, I trudged up the face of the canyon pulling the rope with my weary arms and pushing with my feet.

When her grip loosened, I yelled at her.

"Stay with me, Jack! You hold tight!"

As she tightened her grip and shifted to lock her arms, she whimpered against the pain. Then she rested her head against my neck which sent waves of lightning through my body.

Despite the fire in my weary muscles, I continued to push and pull. Sweat ran down my back and soaked my shirt. The strength faded from my limbs with each movement. I forced my fear down.

"Holt!" I hollered for him around the thirty-foot mark.

He peered over the side and swore.

"Boys, we have to haul them up!"

The rope carried us toward the top of the rim. I held on firmly and I breathed easier when I no longer needed to pull us up.

When we arrived at the gentle slope, the boys hauled us the rest of the way quickly. Once we laid on the flat surface of the canyon rim away from the edge, I nudged Jack, despite the throbbing in my arms.

"You can let go now."

She released her hold and blacked out. I laid there next to her breathing heavily as my arms and legs burned.

"Shoot!" Holt hollered. "Jack ain't a man, is he?"

I shook my head. If I wasn't so exhausted from the strain, I would have been furious.

Charlie slid his hands under Jack's arms and dragged her body further away from the canyon edge. He mopped away the blood from her face with his handkerchief.

Holt helped me to my feet. My legs wobbled, but I

stayed upright.

"We gotta get back to camp," I said.

Then Dustin lifted Jack into his arms. Holt and Charlie packed up our gear and followed behind us.

Jack was a woman. I cursed. There was a woman on my crew. And she was in a bad way.

As I ran a hand through my hair, I realized I lost my hat during the ordeal.

Once we got her back to camp, I assessed her injuries. The rope loosened, and I pulled it from her arm. I unbuttoned her shirt and saw how she wrapped her chest. Before I thought the next action through, I took my knife and sliced the wrap open to reveal her bare chest.

I swallowed hard and closed her shirt before the others saw. Then I took her into my tent and laid her on my pallet. I slid her shirt open on her left side and leaned her toward me. She felt so limp in my arms.

Dark purple bruises covered her dislocated shoulder and arm. What I wouldn't give for my mama's medical knowledge in that moment. We had to get her to a doctor, but dusk already settled over camp. We could only make her comfortable and watch her until morning.

As I buttoned her shirt, I tried to wipe away the image of her soft skin and pleasing curves from my mind. She had disguised her beauty well.

I cursed under my breath again. Jack was a woman. Name probably wasn't even Jack Bennett.

For several minutes, I watched her. Her long hair covered part of her face, so I brushed it away. Her slight frame and odd facial features made sense with the revelation of her secret. I touched the patch of hair on her upper lip and then tugged. It came right off.

I took a shaky breath as my stomach knotted tighter

than the woven cords of a rope.

Jack was a woman. A beautiful woman. A beautiful woman in a camp full of men. Any reputation she once enjoyed would be destroyed.

Heck, a few days ago, I undressed in front of her to go swimming.

My throat constricted. I was not one to feel anxious, but the longer I pondered the situation, my uneasiness increased.

I exited the camp and walked over to my horse, Outlaw, in the makeshift corral. How I longed to ride like the wind to find my way again. Couldn't do it though. As the boss, Jack was my responsibility. I needed to take her to a doctor and deal with the strange turn of events.

"Jack's a woman," Holt said next to me. "You know what that means."

I shook my head.

"One of us has to marry her."

My head snapped up at his suggestion. I frowned.

"She'll be ruined," Holt said. "None of us want that for her."

As my jaw twitched, I followed him back to the fire.

"I'll marry her," Dustin said.

"You?" Charlie scoffed. "This is your first job. How would you provide for her?"

Holt and Charlie were both married with families waiting for them back home. It was me or Dustin. Three pairs of eyes faced me.

"Boone," Holt started.

"Holt, please don't say it." No way was I getting hitched. Much to my mama's dismay, my plan for my life did not include marriage.

"She's close to your age," Charlie said.

"She ain't half bad to look at," Holt said.

"You could provide for her," Dustin said. "You're the boss."

My jaw clenched tighter as I felt like a caged bear. I could not deny their logic. For the reasons they gave, I made the most sense. And I was the one that saw her... I couldn't even think the words.

I cleared my throat and ran a hand through my hair as heaviness pressed on me like a gigantic boulder falling from a cliff, crushing me under its weight.

Finally, I spoke, "We'll pack up in the morning. We're about halfway between Ash Fork and Chino Valley. I'll head south to Chino Valley. You head back up to Ash Fork. Return the mules and ship everything back to Prescott on the train."

I dug in my pocket and counted out a fair amount of cash. I handed it to Holt.

"This should cover the cost of train tickets, rent for the mules, and shipping our supplies. When you arrive in Prescott, deliver the supplies to the office. My brother, James, works at an office across from the town square and can unlock it for you."

Then I stuffed the rest of my money back in my pocket.

"I'll be in touch in soon, since we'll need to come back out and finish the job."

"With Jack, right?" Dustin asked.

I shook my head.

"Dustin, can you help me rig up a litter for Jack's mare? I don't think she'll be able to ride."

"Sure thing, boss."

Since Jack was in my tent, I headed toward hers. Holt jogged up next to me. "Are you gonna do it?"

"What choice do I have?" I growled. Then I ducked into

her tent and laid down on her small pallet.

God, show me what to do. I'm lost.

No answer came back.

CHAPTER II

JACLYN

Just before dawn I woke. I felt around in the darkness. My surroundings were unfamiliar. As I tried to roll onto my left side, pain seared through my shoulder and arm, and I screamed out.

"Jack?"

Boone's voice greeted me from the dark outside.

"What happened?"

"Can I come in?"

"Yes. Where am I?"

"My tent."

My throat constricted, and my breathing grew heavy as I tried to remember how I got there. What had I done?

I moaned.

"Calm down. Don't get up."

"What happened?"

"You almost died, alright!" He yelled at me. "And we know your real name isn't Jack."

I coughed, and my head throbbed.

"Boone," I whispered. "I don't remember. The last thing… I climbed down the rope ladder just past the easy slope."

"What's your name?"

"Jack Bennett."

He sat down next to me and shook me. I cried in pain. "Cut the act. What's your name? Is it even Bennett or did you steal some poor fellow's name?"

In the dark, I clutched my chest. My bindings were gone! I felt my upper lip. No mustache. I touched my hair. I closed my eyes and took a deep breath.

"My name is Jaclyn Bennett. My father is Silas Bennett, the Surveyor General of California."

"Did he send you here?" The acid dripped from his voice.

"No. He probably hasn't discovered that I'm gone yet."

"You've got some nerve, Jaclyn."

I tried to sit up. A hand held my right shoulder in place.

His voice softened. "Don't get up. You have a dislocated shoulder. You hit the side of the canyon wall hard. Your face is beat up. From what I... Your back and shoulder looked bruised."

"You saw it?" I shrieked.

"I needed to assess your condition."

"And I suppose you're the one responsible for my missing bindings."

He cleared his throat. "I'm the only one who saw... Saw anything."

My face heated. "But they know?"

"Yes."

The pounding in my head matched the racing beats of my heart. Boone saw my chest, my back, my shoulder. The crew knew I was a woman. I was finished.

Boone's hand touched the side of my cheek in the dark tent. He smoothed back my hair.

"We'll take care of you, Jaclyn. You have nothing to fear. I'll make sure of it."

The compassion in his voice confused me. Tears welled up and spilled over before I swiped my sleeve across my eyes.

"I'm gonna go. The sun will be up soon. I'll take you to Chino Valley for medical care. We'll talk more."

The tent opening flapped softly back into place. My head hurt so I closed my eyes.

When I woke again, I was on a travois being pulled by a horse.

"Hello?"

The horse stopped.

Boone appeared with a canteen. "You're awake. Thirsty?"

I nodded.

He held the canteen to my lips and tipped it. I drank greedily of the water. When he offered more, I refused.

"We're only a few more hours away from Chino Valley."

Then he sat down on the ground next to me.

"You don't look great. Folks are going to see your face and arm, take a good look at me, and think I did this to you."

I sucked in a sharp breath. "I'm sorry."

"We need a story that is believable. Saying that you were part of a survey crew isn't it."

As my eyes searched his, he looked away.

"Indian attack?"

"I barely have a scratch on me."

"What do we have with us?" I asked.

"My horse. Your slow mare. Our saddlebags."

"Can we pretend we're married?"

His head snapped toward me, and his eyebrows furrowed deeply. "Not when we stand before the preacher and ask him to marry us."

"What are you talking about?"

"Jaclyn, for better or for worse, we're in this together. Looks like we'll start out on the worse side of things."

I tried to sit up.

"Stop being so stubborn and lie still."

"Are you saying you are going to marry me?"

He grunted.

"Do I get a say?"

"Do you want one?"

I growled. "You might be my boss, but you aren't responsible for me."

"If you could see the situation clearly, you would see it's your best option."

He set the canteen next to me. Then he stood.

"If we want to make it before nightfall, we need to go."

Then he disappeared. I heard him cluck to the horses, and we moved forward again.

I sighed.

When I hopped that train for Prescott, I never once considered what would happen if something revealed my identity after spending time at camp with a crew of men. I hadn't worried about it, because Papa took such good care of me on the expeditions he led.

This crew didn't watch me grow up from an awkward tomboy into a woman under my papa's protection. Instead, they were strangers who only met me two weeks ago. I worked alongside them. I saw them jump into a river for a bath, for goodness's sake.

The reality of my circumstance hit me square in the face. I was ruined.

So was Boone. Once word got out that he hired a woman and let her camp out without a husband among a group of men...

He hated me. He had to. I ruined his life.

———

On the way to Chino Valley, I faded in and out of consciousness. Just outside of the town, Boone stopped the horses and came back to talk to me.

"Thought of a good story yet?" he asked as he sat down next to me.

"How about the truth? I fell off the side of a cliff and you rescued me. It's not an awful story. Besides, I doubt anyone will ask."

He stroked his beard. "Fine."

His brilliant blue eyes held a sharp edge as he searched mine. Then he dropped his head into his hands. The muscle in his jaw twitched.

"I never pictured proposing to a woman like this." He lifted his head. "Frankly, I wasn't sure I ever would. But, for your sake I don't see another option."

My heart softened over his sense of duty and honor. I didn't deserve it. I didn't deserve him. A small part of me wanted to be his wife, but, for his sake, I needed to convince him he didn't have to marry me.

"I won't hold it against you if you walk away. This is my mess. It doesn't have to be yours."

"You don't understand. I could not live with myself if I walk away. I'm not sure I can if I go forward with this. It's an impossible situation."

I couldn't fault him for his honesty. In fact, I appreciated it. I reached for his hand and took it in mine.

"If you want to marry me, Boone, then do it. Don't feel like I'm forcing you to. I'm not. But if you do, I promise I will honor those vows. I will treat you with respect and I will do my best to learn to be a good wife."

I didn't want to marry any more than he did. Yet it seemed the most likely path.

He sighed and pulled his hand back.

"Let's get you to the doctor."

Then he disappeared, and the horses led us into town. After a few minutes, they stopped again. He came around to the travois and lifted me into his arms.

My breath caught as tingles traveled along my side and arm where I touched him. Attraction. That's what it was. I could do worse for a husband.

Then he carried me into the doctor's office. The middle-aged doctor led us down the hall to an exam room.

"Her shoulder is dislocated," Boone said.

The doctor looked from him to me and raised an eyebrow.

"I had a nasty fall down the side of a cliff," I said.

"You can wait out front," the doctor said to Boone.

"I'd like to stay if I can," his voice was soft. "She's my wife."

Well, I guess I knew his intention to marry me hadn't changed.

"Please, let him stay," I said. "I could use the support."

The doctor studied us both for a minute. Then he asked me to slide my hurt arm out of the shirtsleeve. Boone held the loose shirtsleeve while I bent my arm. I couldn't move it so, Boone took my elbow and gently tugged the shirt over my shoulder, leaving it draped over my front to keep my modesty intact. His fingers swept my hair to my right side out of the way.

"Bite down on this." The doctor handed me a piece of leather. I did as he asked.

With a surprise sharp movement, he snapped my shoulder back into place. I screamed out. Boone stiffened next to me. Then my body went limp as my vision blurred.

I woke up a minute later.

Boone held my hand. The doctor rolled me onto my side and examined the area. Then he put my arm back in the shirtsleeve and pulled the shirt down over my belly before pressing on it.

"I don't see any signs of internal injuries. Just a lot of bruising and some cuts and scrapes. Lift nothing heavy for a while. Other than that, you should heal up fine."

"Thank you," I said as I sat up.

"Stay here," Boone said as he left. A few minutes later, he came back and lifted me into his arms.

"I can walk."

As he carried me down the street to the hotel, he ignored my statement. He set me in a chair while he paid for a room. Then he picked me up and carried me upstairs to the room.

Once he had the door open, a feat to be sure with me in his arms, he laid me down on the bed.

"You should rest. I'll go take care of the horses and then I'll be back."

My eyes widened.

"We'll marry tomorrow, so I'll sleep on the floor tonight."

As he pulled the door closed behind him, I remembered Papa's conversation with me before I left. He wanted me to settle down and marry. I recognized the irony, though I was certain he never imagined it would happen like it did.

CHAPTER 12

BOONE

When I laid Jaclyn down on the doctor's table, I saw his look of judgment. I was sure he did not believe the cliff story. I hoped my tender care of her changed his opinion. Not that it really mattered. I doubted either of us would see that doctor again.

Claiming her as my wife with my words, I surprised myself. My decision solidified in that moment. It was the right thing to do. So, why did it feel so terrible?

Mama would be livid. As far as she knew, I was supposed to survey Hell Canyon for James and his new railroad for several weeks.

Instead, I'd be home the day before Thanksgiving. Jaclyn and I would be married in a wedding with none of my family. That bothered me. Mama would be disappointed. So would my sister, Violet.

I tried to prepare myself mentally for questions from my family, and I anticipated a trip to the barn for a stern lecture from Papa.

As I led the horses to the livery, I ground my teeth. I paid the livery owner and told him I'd pick them up in the morning. After I slung our saddlebags over each shoulder, I walked back to the hotel room.

Jaclyn slept soundly as I entered the room. After grabbing the extra pillow off the bed, I turned down the lamp and laid down on the floor between the bed and the door.

Marrying Jaclyn wouldn't be so bad, I tried to convince myself. She was beautiful. Smart. We worked well together. I would miss her on the job. She was a tremendous asset in the field.

I ran a hand through my hair and rolled onto my back as I stared at the ceiling. The woman I was about to marry lied to me and pretended to be a man. Nothing about it felt right. Taking any other course of action felt worse.

When Sam married Ellie Mae three years ago, I was there. I remembered the vows. 'Til death do us part. For better or for worse. A lifetime commitment should not be hastily made.

I wasn't the first man to face such a dilemma. That knowledge didn't make me feel any better as I was the one who would bear the burden.

The next morning, I rose after only a few hours of sleep. Jaclyn did not rouse, so I left to find a preacher.

There was one church in town. When I entered the building, I found the preacher in an office off the main sanctuary.

"Morning, pastor," I said after I introduced myself. "My fiancée and I were wondering if you would marry us today."

The pastor introduced himself as Pastor Joe. "Are you sure you don't want to plan something with family present?"

"No. She almost died the other day and neither one of us want to wait." The string of minor lies pressed on my heart.

I shook it off.

"Alright. When did you want to marry?"

"I just need to fetch her from the hotel."

He agreed to wait there, so I went back to the hotel. Jaclyn woke as I entered the room.

"How are you feeling?"

"Sore. Like I fell off a cliff."

I snorted at her joke.

"Pastor Joe is waiting at the church if you're ready."

"I…" She sighed. "I wish I had a dress."

"I brought your saddlebag."

She shook her head. "My only dress is in a trunk back in Prescott. I didn't want to chance being discovered." She stood. "It doesn't matter. Let's go."

I picked up our saddlebags.

"Are you sure you're feeling up to it?"

Jaclyn scoffed. "Change your mind?"

"No."

Then she took my arm, and we left the room. I returned the key at the front desk before I accompanied her to the church. My heart thudded slowly at first. The closer we got, the more it pounded.

When we stood before Pastor Joe, he hesitated and looked over Jaclyn's bruises and cuts. I knew he thought I hurt her. As his eyes traveled the length of me, I forced a cheerful smile.

At length Pastor Joe led us in our vows, and I promised many things that my heart did not feel. Things that required effort to keep.

As she repeated her vows, Jaclyn smiled up at me. She was more sincere than me.

"Do you have a ring?" Pastor Joe asked.

I shook my head. He skipped that part and announced

we were husband and wife.

"You may kiss your bride."

I froze. I blinked. My throat constricted, and my heart squeezed tight at the thought of kissing her. When Jaclyn tugged on my arm, I finally leaned down and brushed a kiss on her cheek.

The pastor completed a marriage license and handed it to me. I was certain Mama would need to see it to believe it.

Then we headed to the livery. We waited as the livery owner saddled our horses before we rode back to Prescott.

Once we arrived in Prescott, I went to the boardinghouse to retrieve Jack Bennett's trunk which I brought to my office. Then I took her slow mare back to the livery where I rented it.

When I returned to the office, Jaclyn wore a stylish purple silk dress. It showed off her womanly figure. My breath stopped as I watched her wind her long, silky black hair into a knot at the base of her neck. Her graceful, beckoning neck. If she wore that dress during our wedding, I would not have hesitated to kiss her thoroughly.

I cleared my throat.

"Boone, thank you for everything," she said as she pinned a matching hat on her head before sitting in the chair across from my desk.

"Now what?" she asked.

"We go home."

I took a pitcher of water and the washbasin to the back room.

"Where is home?"

I undressed and splashed water over my face, neck, and chest. "Colter Ranch."

"You live on a ranch?"

"We live on a ranch," I growled.

After I dried off using my dirty shirt, I donned a fresh shirt and trousers which I left at the office. I knew Mama would be unhappy if I showed up trail dirty.

"Oh, right."

I ran a hand through my wet hair which reminded me I lost my hat.

"Let's stop at the mercantile before we head home. I need a new hat."

When I emerged from the back room, she smiled.

"You look refreshed."

I grunted. "Let's go."

"Boone! I thought I saw Outlaw—" My brother, Sam enter-ed the building and stopped short when he saw I was not alone. "Oh, who's this?"

"Jaclyn, this is my older brother, Sam. Sam, meet my wife, Jaclyn."

"Wife?!" Sam's eyes grew so wide I thought they might roll right out of his head. "Did you finish the Hell Canyon survey?"

Jaclyn stood next to me and flashed him a charming smile. "A pleasure to meet you, Sam. We're headed to the mercantile."

Sam blinked as he raised an eyebrow.

My stomach knotted as I headed for the front door, and I locked it behind us.

"You're in luck, if you want to ride back with me," Sam said. "I just purchased some supplies. Got the wagon with me. I mean if Jaclyn wants to ride back…"

"Thank you so much," she said as I stiffened. "I would appreciate that since I don't own a horse."

"Come," I said gruffly as I tugged her forward.

"We'll be back shortly," she said over her shoulder. "That was rude, Boone."

I didn't really care.

When we entered the mercantile, I asked if she needed anything.

"I… um.."

"Spit it out, Jack," I grumbled. "Jaclyn."

"I only have," she lowered her voice, "men's clothes."

I held back a curse. Seemed too many curses were on the tip of my tongue in the last few days. It wasn't like me.

"Can I get one work dress? Then I'll save up for more later."

"How?" The word was out of my mouth before I could re-tract it.

Her shoulders slumped. "Right. I won't have a job or in-come."

"Get what you need," I said through gritted teeth.

As I perused the hats, my jaw twitched. I loved my old, white cowboy hat. Replacing it was a symbol of the dra-matic changes in my life. I finally settled on a new white hat that resembled my old one. I frowned, knowing how much I hated breaking in a new hat.

Then I walked the aisles until I found Jaclyn. When I found her, she carried two ready-made work dresses in her arms. Once she spotted me, she lifted the hem of her purple skirt to reveal her field boots.

"Get some shoes, too."

She handed me the dresses. I flinched and snapped my jaw shut. The clerk helped her find the right size.

"Anything else, dear?" I asked with dripping sarcasm.

Jaclyn shrunk back. "No. That will suffice for now."

I paid for the purchases and waited for the clerk to wrap Jaclyn's items in brown paper. Then I escorted her back to the office.

When Sam spotted us, he pulled the wagon in front of

the building. I helped Jaclyn up onto the seat next to him. Then I tossed our purchases in the back. I loaded our saddlebags and her trunk in the back of the wagon. Then I mounted Outlaw, and we headed for home.

Dread filled the bottom of my stomach as the day was far from over and I still had to face Mama.

CHAPTER 13

JACLYN

"Thank you so much, Sam. How fortuitous that you could help us," I said as I watched Boone ride ahead of the wagon.

"No trouble," Sam replied.

"Boone has said little about his family. Do you have other siblings?" My heart raced. I needed some information before we arrived at the ranch.

Sam cleared his throat. "There's five of us men. And my brother-in-law, Grady. Then my little sister, Violet. We call her Vi."

"Five?" My voice squeaked.

"James is the oldest. He lives in town and works for the railroad. Then there's me. My wife and I live in the old ranch house with our two boys, Sterling and Brody. Boone is the middle one. Then Deacon and Preston."

"And your parents?" I wondered if they were still alive.

"Mama's name is Hannah. Papa's Will. I'm sure Mama will be happy if you call her Mama. Ellie Mae, my wife, does."

I kept my jaw from slacking. Boone's family was enormous.

"My Aunt Julia and her husband, Adam, live at the ranch too. Their youngest daughter, Dory, still lives at home. The other two are married now."

As the silence stretched on, I thought through what to say.

"When did you get married?" Sam asked.

I swallowed the lump in my throat. "This morning."

"When did you meet? How long have you known each other? Boone said nothing about a sweetheart in town."

I rested my hand at my throat. "I… We met right before the surveying trip."

"Hmm."

I didn't dare say more. Boone needed to choose how he explained my sudden appearance to his family.

"Boone's done some crazy things in his time," Sam muttered. He didn't finish the thought. He didn't have to. Clearly, my marriage to his brother shocked him.

When we crested the top of a hill, I scanned the valley below.

"It's lovely."

"That it is. Never tire of seeing the place from this vantage point."

So many buildings filled the valley. A shimmering blue lake butted up against a series of granite rock formations and the foothills of a mountain.

"A mile," I mumbled.

"Pardon?"

"I'm good at estimating distances. The lake at its longest point is one mile."

Sam shrugged. "If you say so."

As Sam pulled the wagon to a stop near the barn, Boone reined in his black stallion. He looped the reins over a post before he helped me down. When his hands clasped my waist, my stomach fluttered. He let his hands linger for a minute after lowering my feet to the ground. As my pulse raced, I smiled up at him. When he released me and turned to unload my things from the wagon, I missed the feel of his hands on my waist.

"Wait here. It's best if I introduce you to Mama."

While he cared for his horse, I stood and waited by my trunk and our things. When he joined me, I carried my purchases and saddlebag. He dropped his saddlebag on top of my trunk and hefted it to his shoulder as if it were as light as a cloud. He took my free hand in his and laced his fingers with mine, catching me off guard.

A short woman with graying strawberry blond hair flew out of the yellow house.

"Boone? You're home?"

When she noticed me, she stopped short. She tilted her head to one side and pursed her lips. Her eyebrows squished together.

"Mama."

He let go of my hand before he set my trunk down on the porch. Then he took my things from me and placed them on top of my trunk.

"This is my wife, Jaclyn."

"Wife? What do you mean wife?"

"Hannah," I said drawing her attention. "It's a pleasure to meet you."

"Oh. Um." She straightened her back and smiled warmly at me. "So nice to meet you, Jaclyn."

Then she frowned at Boone, and I felt the tension between them. I wondered how many more times a similar scene would play out before us.

"Have you been traveling long?" she asked as she accompanied me into the house. "Should I fix you something to tide you over until supper?"

I glanced at Boone.

"Yes, Mama, that would be nice. We've been on the road since early this morning."

"Have a seat, Jaclyn," she said. "It won't take me but a minute."

"Can I help?"

"Oh, no."

Boone squeezed my shoulder. Then he retrieved the trunk and carried it upstairs. He made a second trip up with the rest of our things.

My palms sweat and I wiped them on my skirt as I took a seat at the large oak dining table. He lived in his parent's house. We lived with his parents. I don't know what I expected, but not that.

"Boone!" Hannah hollered with a tinge of anger. "Food is ready."

He hurried downstairs and into the dining room.

"Sorry."

As he took a seat next to me, Hannah set a few sandwiches on the table along with two glasses of water.

"If you'll excuse me," she said as she smiled at me. Then she glowered at Boone. "I need to go speak to your father."

Boone shifted in his chair.

As soon as she left the house, he reached for a sandwich.

"How much trouble are you in?" I asked.

"Dunno." He stuffed half of the sandwich in his mouth.

"I'm sorry."

He swallowed and turned toward me. "What's done is done. Best if we try to move forward. Stop looking back."

His voice sounded sullen. So different from the animated storyteller at camp or the exuberant swimmer or the joyous nature-lover or the studious surveyor. Sullen didn't fit the Boone I knew.

"Eat up."

I took a bite of a sandwich. Then another. The reality of our choices finally caught up to me. I was Boone's wife. His surprise, unexpected wife. I needed to work hard to keep his family from feeling alienated.

After I finished my sandwich, I drank the water. When I stood, my knees buckled, and Boone caught me. I cried out when he wrenched my shoulder.

"Are you alright?" he asked as he held me close.

"Just exhausted." I clung to him as my energy faded.

"I'll show you my... Our room."

He helped me climb the stairs and guided me down the hall to his bedroom.

"It's not much. I hadn't planned for... We'll figure out a long-term plan soon."

He led me to the bed and held out his hand.

"Your hat."

I took it off and handed it to him. When I bent down to untie my shoes, I groaned at the pain. Then he kneeled in front of me and took my booted foot in his hand. He untied my boots and slid them off. I felt so unworthy of his kindness. A tear slid from the corner of my eye before I wiped it away.

"It's been a long day."

"Yes. And you need some rest. It was only two days ago that you..." He cleared his throat. "I'll see if Mama can make some willow bark tea. Then I'll bring it up."

After I removed the pins from my hair, he took them and set them on a dresser as I laid down. Then he closed the door behind him as I fell asleep, despite my worry and guilt.

CHAPTER 14

BOONE

When I returned downstairs, I set some water on the stove to boil. I could only imagine what Jaclyn thought. At least Mama was kind to her. I knew a trip to the barn was in my near future.

As a boy, whenever I got in trouble, Papa took me to the barn. Sometimes I received a stern scolding. Sometimes wise counsel. Other times, my punishment was mucking stalls or some other annoying chore. I wondered how many stalls it would take to atone for coming home with a bruised wife.

I sighed heavily. At least the house was quiet. Deacon and Grady were still at work. Preston was probably out with the herd or half-drunk somewhere. Vi was likely on her way home from school in town.

The responsibility of leading a crew of my own was challenging, but it seemed like nothing compared to coming home with a wife.

A wife.

Shaking my head, I moved the boiling kettle to the back burner and found a mug. I didn't know how to make the tea, so I waited for Mama.

Just then, she opened the door. Her cheeks flushed red,

and she sighed loudly.

"Mama, can you make some willow bark tea for Jaclyn? She's in a lot of pain from the fall."

When she frowned at me, I realized she did not know what I meant. She moved to retrieve the willow bark. Then she let it steep in the hot water in the mug.

"I'll take it up to her," I said.

"When you're done, come out to the barn. Your father and I want to speak with you, and we don't want any interruptions as your brothers and sister come home."

"Yes, Mama."

I took the warm mug upstairs. Even though I hated to wake Jaclyn, I knew the medicine would ease her pain.

"Jack," I whispered. "Jaclyn."

She opened her eyes, and I helped her sit up.

"Drink this. It'll lessen the pain."

She sipped on it.

"Will you be alright? My parents want to talk to me."

She nodded. "Go."

"I'll be out at the barn. You may hear some noise as my siblings come home. Just rest. Don't feel compelled to come down for supper if you aren't feeling up to it."

"Alright."

She looked at me with her mismatched eyes. The urge to kiss her forehead was too strong, so I did before I left the room.

The walk to the barn felt like a hundred yard climb up a cliff with a nasty overhang and few holds. Vi greeted me with a hug before she bounded into the house while I forced my feet forward.

"Boone." Papa's voice was strained. "Your mother tells me you brought home a wife?"

"Yes."

"With cuts and bruises on her face."

I closed my eyes. Did they not know me at all? I would never hurt a woman.

"I can explain."

"I should hope so," Mama interjected.

"Hannah, let him speak."

Mama took a seat on a stool at Papa's workbench and folded her arms over her chest as a scowl settled on her face.

I took a deep breath. Then I told them everything. How I hired Jack to be my assistant surveyor. How none of the crew knew she wasn't what she claimed to be.

"I mean, she's a great surveyor. She can do complicated math in her head. You should see her maps."

"Get to the part about why she's injured and how she ended up married to you," Papa said as he crossed his arms over his chest.

"We were climbing over the edge of the canyon two days ago."

It seemed longer than that. Much longer.

"I had every confidence that he… She could do the job. She shot a deer for us just a few days before. Everything she did, she did well. None of us thought she was a woman."

In hindsight, her reaction to the swim should have been a clue. I never contemplated that she was a woman. My hands sweat so I wiped them on my trousers before I continued.

"We took the normal precautions. I know you think I'm reckless, but with my job and my crew, we take appropriate safety measures. She was clearly familiar with them."

Mama wrung her hands. Papa's furrowed brow and narrowed eyes warned me to get on with the story.

"The short version is that she lost her footing, dislocated her shoulder, and hit the canyon wall pretty hard. Hard enough to knock her out. She almost..." My voice cracked. "We almost lost her."

Emotion sprang up unexpectedly, and I coughed to stuff it away, afraid of what she really meant to me.

"I roused her and got her to hold on to me as I climbed sixty feet up the side of the cliff. It was during that process that I became aware she was a woman."

As the fear from that day vise-gripped my heart, I cleared my throat.

"Once we were safely at the top, I checked her injuries. If I wasn't sure before then, I had no doubts at that point."

"What do you mean, Boone?" Mama's voice accused me.

"Does it matter?"

I paced back and forth in front of them.

"When she almost died, her secret was revealed. I only had one honorable choice, and it is what I chose. I brought her to Chino Valley, to a doctor, and we married there this morning."

Mama gasped.

Papa frowned. "Marriage is a vow before God."

"Don't you think I know that? I said the vow and I will keep it."

Papa shook his head. "Boone."

I heard the disappointment in his voice. I ground my teeth as my blood boiled.

"I did the right thing. The honorable thing. The sacrificial thing to protect her and her future."

The silence stretched. I wanted to run away or ride like the wind through valleys and mountains. Far from the turmoil simmering inside of me.

"What did the doctor say?" Mama asked calmly as her shoulders sagged.

"She dislocated her shoulder. He set it. No internal injuries that he could tell. She hit the side of the wall hard. She's resting now."

"I should go," Mama said. "It's time to start supper, but I'll check on her first."

Then mama slid from the stool and left the barn.

"Sit."

I took the seat that Mama vacated as I faced Papa.

He let out a long breath. "I wish you would not have rushed into marriage."

As I crossed my arms over my chest, I frowned, annoyed that Papa failed to see the good in my choice.

"Marriage is for a lifetime. There may have been other options. Does she have family?"

"Her father is in California."

"Does he know what she did?"

I shook my head. "She said she left while he was on a surveying trip."

"Ah. So, she learned the trade from him."

I nodded.

Papa's shoulders slumped as he wiped a hand over his face. "I know it was a tough decision."

Finally, he acknowledged what I did. I uncrossed my arms and sat up straighter.

"I probably would have made the same decision in your position."

When he locked his eyes on mine, I swallowed hard.

"Marriage is serious. It's hard. Starting one like you and Jaclyn have... It won't be easy. You barely know each other. There will be temptation to resent her for your choice to marry her. You need to work twice as hard to learn about her and how to love her."

I didn't fully understand what he tried to tell me, but I nodded my head, anyway.

"You run, but you can't run from your wife. It will only make you both miserable. There is no honor in it."

"Understood."

After a few minutes, he asked, "Have you thought about where you'll live?"

"Not yet. I should probably get us a place in town."

"Well, stay here through the weekend. Tomorrow is Thanksgiving. The whole family will be here. You should prepare her for questions."

Deacon entered the barn, shuffling his feet loudly. "Mama said supper is almost ready."

As we followed him back to the house, I felt the weight of the world pressing down on my shoulders.

When I noticed Jaclyn wasn't in the dining room, I went upstairs to see how she felt. She stirred as I entered.

"Mama said supper is ready. Do you feel up to meeting my brothers and sister?"

"I suppose."

My gaze darted to the corner of the room as my throat constricted. "I won't lie. It's going to be very awkward. Maybe even tense."

"I understand."

As I waited for her to fix her hair, I sat on the edge of the bed. When she reached down for her shoes, I stopped her.

"No need. No one will see your feet."

She snorted. "I suppose not."

Then I helped her downstairs to meet the rest of my family as lead filled my stomach.

CHAPTER 15

JACLYN

The tender side of Boone Colter comforted me. He treated me so well from the moment we set foot on the ranch. He took my hand as we descended the stairs and entered the dining room.

By the time we arrived, no two seats were beside each other.

Boone stood by his sister. "Would you mind giving Jaclyn your chair?"

She moved to the empty seat across the table.

Before he held out a chair for me, he introduced me.

"This is my wife, Jaclyn Bennett." He closed his eyes. "Colter."

His brother Deacon stood and shook my hand while he introduced himself. Then Grady did the same.

"I'm not a Colter," Grady explained. "My sister brought me here after our parents passed. Though the Colters are like family now." He smiled.

"This is Violet," Boone said pointing to his sister. "We call her Vi."

"Nice to meet you, Jaclyn." She giggled. "Now I have

two sisters."

Boone half smiled. "That you do."

Only one brother remained seated. He wouldn't look at me.

"Preston," Will said with an edge to his voice.

Preston nodded at me.

Boone held out a chair, and I sat. Then he sat to my left.

"Where's Sam and his family?" Boone asked.

"He said Ellie Mae wanted a quiet meal at home tonight," Hannah said.

I glanced at Boone. His jaw tightened. I guessed I was the reason they stayed home and that it was unusual.

Will cleared his throat and bowed his head. The rest of the family complied as he prayed. He thanked God for the addition of me to the Colter family.

When I sucked in a sharp breath of air, Boone clasped my hand under the table and rubbed his thumb over my knuckles. I blinked back tears. Boone said he told his parents everything. I didn't understand how they could be thankful for me.

Once Will closed the prayer, everyone said, "Amen."

As the family passed food around the table, I took a platter from Boone with my left hand and winced as pain shot up my arm. My cheeks flamed when I almost dropped it. He tightened his grip and served me instead. Then he handed it across the table to Vi.

Deacon noticed every detail of what happened. He said nothing.

"What happened to your face?" Vi asked.

The table silenced as all eyes turned toward me.

"She—" Boone started to explain.

"I was helping Boone survey a canyon, and I lost my footing." I winked at her. "My face stopped my fall."

Boone snorted.

"My shoulder helped, too. Dislocated it. So, I'm not feeling one hundred percent. Maybe more like eighty-seven percent."

Vi's eyes went wide.

Boone chuckled. "So precise," he said under his breath.

It was good to see a glimpse of my Boone. The cheerful one.

"How was school?" I asked her to take the attention off me.

Thankfully, she launched into a detailed explanation about a young boy who picked on her in school.

"You know he likes you," Grady teased.

Her cheeks turned rosy.

"She's twelve," Boone whispered for my benefit.

When I picked up my fork and knife, my left arm hurt so I picked at the mashed potatoes instead.

"Here," Boone said as he slid my plate closer to him. He cut up the meat for me.

Everyone listened to Grady as he told a story about his job with the local vet. If anyone noticed my discomfort, they hid it well.

Boone slid my plate back in front of me.

"Thank you."

Before finishing her meal, Hannah stood and brewed some tea. Then she set it in front of me.

"That should help," she said.

I sipped the bitter liquid. Willow bark tea. I smiled in her direction as she took her seat again.

"Jaclyn, where are you from?" Hannah asked.

I swallowed a bite of food.

"From Sacramento. My father is the Surveyor General for the state. After my mother passed when I was fourteen, I apprenticed with him."

Hannah cleared her throat. "So, you were a surveyor, too?"

"Assistant Surveyor, yes. For six years."

Boone shifted in his seat next to me. "She's good at it."

His compliment warmed my heart.

"Her maps are flawless."

I glanced up at him. The admiration in his eyes warmed my heart.

"That's as long as Boone has been surveying," Hannah said.

"Yes, I know."

I was not sure what Hannah's angle was. I could not decide if she was trying to learn about me or trying to trip me up.

"How did the two of you meet?" Preston asked as he sat up straighter and leaned forward in his chair. He narrowed his eyes at Boone.

Boone frowned. "She was my assistant surveyor on the trip to Hell Canyon."

Deacon shifted in his chair. Grady's mouth dropped open for a second. Vi's eyes went wide. Will and Hannah did not react.

Preston pressed Boone for more information. "You hired a woman?"

"Leave it." Boone warned him.

Preston snorted. "Not a chance. Spill it."

Boone stood and rounded the corner of the table. He grabbed Preston by his arms and hauled him out of the house. I swallowed hard, not sure what happened.

Deacon stood.

"Sit," Will said. "Let them work it out between them."

Deacon settled back in his chair.

I pushed my plate away. The willow bark tea numbed some of the pain and brought exhaustion with it. I didn't know what to do. I wanted to go upstairs to bed. But I didn't want to upset Boone if he expected me to be there when he returned.

"Dessert?" Hannah asked as she stood and cleared away the plates. Vi helped her.

When I tried to rise, she placed a hand on my shoulder.

"Please, take it easy. I know you're still recovering."

She and Vi set a plate of apple pie in front of everyone at the table. I declined. They set one out for Boone and Preston.

We could hear their loud voices for a few minutes before the sound grew more distant. Everyone hurried through their dessert before retiring to the parlor.

"Let me mix up a salve for those scrapes," Hannah said.

"I don't want to be a bother."

"It's no trouble."

"Mama knows a lot about medicine and doctoring," Vi explained. "She fixes up all kinds of things. She even stitched up Papa's leg a few years back when our bull gouged his leg."

"Vi, Jaclyn doesn't need to hear about that."

Within a few minutes, she made a sticky paste. When she sat in the chair next to me, I turned to face her. She dabbed the paste on the cuts on my face.

"There. That should help them heal faster."

She wiped the excess from her finger onto her apron. Then she took my hand in hers.

"I know tonight was awkward. We were all shocked that Boone came home with a wife. Coming home with a pet bear, would have made more sense to us."

I glanced down at the table.

"Jaclyn, you are welcome here. Give the family time to get to know you and you will feel at home."

"I'm sorry." My tears fell.

"This is all my fault. When I disguised myself as a man, I never thought…" My voice caught. I looked up at her. "I spent six years doing the same job as a woman with my papa. It never occurred to me what the consequences might be if I was discovered. I'm so sorry I did this to your son."

"Jack." Boone's voice came from the doorway. "Jaclyn, you didn't do this to me. We talked about this. It was my decision."

She released my hands and stood. She patted my shoulder and left.

I hid my face with my hands and sobbed. He came and sat next to me and rested an arm on my shoulders.

"I'm so sorry I ruined your life."

"Hush."

When he nudged me closer, I placed my arms around his waist and rested my head against his chest. I sobbed to release all the pain, fear, and anxiety of the last few days.

"I hope you can forgive me," I said.

He rubbed his hand on my back in soothing circles.

When I finally calmed, he said, "Go on up to bed. You need some rest."

I leaned my head back to look into his eyes. Moisture glassed over those blue eyes.

"Go. I'm going for a ride."

"In the dark?"

"The moon is full. It will light my way. I'll be back soon."

He stood and held my chair. I stood and trudged up to our room. I changed into my nightgown and slipped beneath the covers before sleep washed over me.

CHAPTER 16

BOONE

"You hired a woman?"

I was in no mood for Preston's goading. I would not air Jaclyn's deception and my mistake in front of the entire family. My parents knew the story. No one else needed to.

"Leave it."

"Not a chance. Spill it."

I stood and was next to Preston in three steps. I hauled him outside. Once the door closed behind us, I shoved him to the ground.

"What the h—!"

"You will not speak ill of my wife!"

Preston stood and dusted the dirt from his pants. He pulled a flask from his vest pocket and took a swig before returning it to his vest. Then he laughed hysterically.

"The mighty Boone Colter! How far you've fallen. Not so perfect now, are you?" He stepped closer and pushed my chest. I grabbed his wrist.

"You hired a woman and now she's trapped you in a marriage."

After I threw his arms away from me, he straightened his back. He was still several inches shorter than me.

"Some tough life you have!" he yelled in my face.

I grabbed his shirt collar and dragged him toward the barn out of the hearing of the family. Of Jaclyn.

Once we were in the barn, he squared off against me. I widened my stance, ready to defend myself if he started throwing his fists at me.

Instead, he poked my chest.

"You finally made a big mistake and you still come out shining." Preston spat the words out. "You get fronted the money from the golden boy to start your own business. Then you hire a woman and get saddled with her as a wife."

He poked my chest again. I leaned forward. The muscles in my arms twitched as my blood boiled.

He scoffed. "Yet, she turns out to be beautiful. Couldn't marry a homely woman. Nope. Not Boone Colter."

"What is your problem?"

Preston stepped back and paced the length of the open area of the barn.

"You. My problem is you. You never fail at anything. Everyone sees you and exalts you. And James and Sam."

He raised his hands in the air and let them fall to his side.

"I'm the forgotten son. No one even knows I'm here. Heck, even Deacon and Grady—he's not even our blood—are respected in this house. Vi is Papa's favorite. Sam is Mama's. Me? Who the heck am I?"

Once I realized Preston's tirade had nothing to do with me, I took a deep breath. I tilted my head from one side to the other to stretch my neck muscles.

"No one would notice if I wasn't here."

I closed my eyes. Then I opened them again.

"What do you want Preston? You want to fight? You want to run? What?"

"Forget you. I'm going into town."

He saddled his liver chestnut stallion, Ranger. Then he rode off to town.

As the weight on my shoulders pressed heavier, I plodded back to the house. I needed to ride, but Papa's caution not to run away from my wife rang in my ears.

When I opened the door to the house, I saw Jaclyn crying. She apologized to my mama. As she heaped the blame on herself, I took that burden from her and added it to my own.

Mama left us alone, and I soothed Jaclyn.

"I'm going for a ride. I'll be back soon."

After Jaclyn climbed the stairs out of sight, I went back to the barn. I saddled Outlaw. Then I pointed him out toward the herd. The sun set hours earlier, but the moon lit my way.

I kicked Outlaw into a full gallop. As we had done countless times over the years, we rode faster than the wind itself. The emotions and stress churning in my soul scared me. I leaned closer to Outlaw's neck, and he gave me even more speed. He understood me.

When he started to lather, I slowed his pace to a gentle walk. Then I dismounted, and I found a small boulder to use as a seat. I rubbed my hand on Outlaw's face.

I thought I was falling in love with my wife. It was a good thing. I wanted to make her my wife in every way and that thought terrified me. If I gave her my heart, she could destroy me.

My vows taunted me. I promised to cherish her. To love her. To have and hold her. In sickness and in health. I promised to do so with God as my witness.

If I allowed her into my heart, I would have to change. I couldn't live recklessly any longer. I would have to consider her needs and desires.

When it came to surveying, I knew I should not allow her to go out in the field anymore. It wasn't safe.

But we were a great team, and I wanted Jaclyn with me at work and at home. She was an excellent surveyor. She made me better at my job and I didn't want to lose that.

The anguish settled deep in my bones. I stood and yelled into the night, releasing the frustration from my soul.

As far as marriage went, I wanted ours to be happy. Like Mama and Papa. Or Sam and Ellie Mae. Jaclyn opened a whole new side of me I didn't know existed. Regardless of why we married, she was the perfect woman for me. Smart. Beautiful. Tough.

I snorted.

Goodness, she was tough. I laughed as I remembered her trying to lug that heavy deer behind her. She was determined to haul it up the canyon.

Images from the accident pushed forward in my mind. She almost died.

The air left my lungs in a whoosh as I sat down on the rock. I rested my head in my hands. I almost lost her before I got to know her.

Lord, what do I do?

Silence.

Sometimes I wondered if He only spoke to good people like my parents. I experienced nothing I would call a clear direction from God. I wished He'd tell me how to move forward as a husband and leader.

Discouraged, I shook it off. Then I mounted Outlaw and headed home. After I finished caring for him, I washed up at the water pump outside despite the chill in the air.

When I entered the house, it was dark, so I went upstairs. The soft glow of the lantern greeted me as I opened the bedroom door. Jaclyn laid on her right side with the covers pulled up to her chin. Her face looked so peaceful.

I undressed and turned down the light. Then I slid into the bed with my back to her.

"Boone?"

My breath vanished, and my pulse quickened. It was the first time someone said my name with hope.

"Yes."

"Would you hold me?"

I rolled over and scooted next to her. Her cotton night-gown felt soft against my skin as she pressed her back closer to me. My mouth went dry as her silky hair brushed against my bare chest. I rested my arm over her waist and held her. Then I fell asleep with my wife in my arms.

The next morning, I woke as light filled the room.

"Are we really married? Did that happen?"

I opened my eyes. Jaclyn sat in her nightgown with her legs crossed. Her hair rested over her shoulder and flowed halfway down her front. The glow in her eyes made me smile.

Then I sat up and matched her posture. I pointed a thumb over my shoulder. "I've got the paper that proves it in my pants."

She nodded. Then she looked down. Pink colored her cheeks.

"You're um... Not wearing anything."

I grinned as I pulled the covers over my lap. "I thought we established that I'm your husband."

"I... I don't know what I expected."

I lifted my hand and trailed a finger down the side of her cheek and her neck. When her breath caught, I placed my hand on the back of her neck and gently guided her face closer to mine. I stopped an inch from her lips as I studied her amber eye. Then her green eye. Hmm. I did like that about her.

Then I kissed her softly on the lips. She tasted sweet like honey. Though I longed to kiss her more passionately, I held back knowing she'd need more time to feel comfortable with me.

When I ended the kiss, she sighed and opened her eyes. Yeah, she liked it, I thought as I released my hold on her.

"You better get dressed," I said. "Mama doesn't like when we're late for breakfast."

"I'm sorry, Boone."

I placed my finger on her lips. "No more apologies. We're in this together."

She nodded. "I'll do my best to win your family over."

"Just be yourself."

Then she slid from the bed and unwrapped one dress she bought yesterday. While her back was turned to me, I dressed for the day. Even though I wanted to watch her, I didn't.

"See you at breakfast," I said as I closed the door behind me.

When I arrived in the dining room, Mama sat at the table and sipped a cup of coffee. No one else was up yet. She smiled when she saw me. I motioned for her to stay seated, and I poured myself a cup of coffee before I sat across from her.

She took something from her apron pocket and slid it across the table. When she moved her hand back, my jaw went slack. A gold wedding band.

"Mama?"

"It was from my first husband."

"The doctor?"

She nodded. "I noticed Jaclyn didn't have a ring on her finger. It makes little sense for me to hold on to it. That was so long ago."

"Are you sure?"

"Yes. You can't tell her or anyone where it came from."

"I'll tell her it is a family heirloom." It was. "And not to make my brothers jealous."

"Ah, there's the Boone I remember." She squeezed my hand.

"She's quite lovely. I hope you find happiness with her."

"Thank you, Mama."

While Mama started cooking breakfast, I stood and went back upstairs. I knocked softly on the door.

Jaclyn opened it a crack. "You don't have to knock on your own door."

She held it open.

"I have something for you."

Her eyes lit with excitement.

Then I held up the ring. "It's a family heirloom, but you can't say anything. Mama doesn't want us to make my brothers jealous."

When she smiled, I slid it onto her finger. My breath quickened as she launched herself into my arms.

"Thank you."

As she pulled back, I held her loosely. Then she placed a hand on my cheek. I lowered my lips to hers for a sweet kiss which she returned. After a moment, I ended the thrilling kiss.

"I'm starving." My voice sounded husky to my ears.

Then I held her hand in mine and led her downstairs for breakfast before I entertained other ideas of how to spend the morning with my wife.

CHAPTER 17

JACLYN

Throughout the morning, I kept looking at the ring on my finger. I liked the reminder that I was married. My heart warmed as I barely believed the Colters would grace me with a family heirloom.

After breakfast, Hannah and Vi prepared a dozen dishes for Thanksgiving. I helped peel potatoes and other tasks that didn't strain my shoulder.

"Hello!" a woman entered the house with arms full of food and a toddler trailing behind.

"Ellie Mae," Vi greeted her. "Let me take that from you."

As Vi set the dish on the table, Ellie Mae smiled and walked toward me. I stood.

"You must be Jaclyn. I'm Sam's wife, Ellie Mae." She held her arms open wide. I accepted the hug and felt more at home.

"Nice to meet you."

"I have several more dishes and a baby. Anyone want to help bring things over?" she asked.

"I can help," I said.

"Let me help," Boone volunteered.

"How's your shoulder?" he asked as we followed Ellie Mae across the yard to her house.

"A little sore."

"Don't carry anything too heavy," he warned as we entered her house.

Sam greeted us before he handed Boone two chairs. "I think we'll need these. Hopefully, we can all squeeze around Mama's table."

"Here," Ellie Mae said as she handed me two pies. "That should be light enough."

It was.

When she picked up a heavier pot, Sam took it from her and nodded toward the baby. She lifted her son from the cradle and carried him close.

We walked back across the yard to the big ranch house. We set the food on the table, except Hannah placed the pies on the counter in the kitchen. Boone slid the two extra chairs around the table.

Then I helped Vi set the table. She took the plates, and I laid out the silverware.

"Is James bringing anyone?" Sam asked.

"I don't think so," Hannah said as she counted the chairs. Then she smiled at me. "Although I wouldn't mind another surprise like Jaclyn."

When I realized she teased, I laughed.

"Will, I think I might need a bigger table soon," she said to her husband.

He chuckled. "Not sure a bigger one would fit."

After a tense supper the night before, his laughter put me at ease.

"I think we're almost ready," Hannah said. "Just waiting on James."

"Where's Preston?" Grady asked.

"He arrived home very late," Deacon said. "I'll go fetch him."

When he returned, a rough-looking Preston walked outside. He came back with wet hair and his shirt half soaked.

James entered shortly after him. He stopped short when he saw Boone with his arm around me.

"Aren't you supposed to be on an expedition?" James frowned as he stood in front of Boone.

"Good to see you, James," Boone replied as he held out a chair for me. Then he sat next to me. James took the seat across from Boone.

It was a tight fit, but we all sat around the table. After Will said grace, Vi started the conversation.

"I am thankful for," she said. Then she stopped to explain the family tradition to me. "We all say something we're thankful for."

I nodded.

"I'm thankful for a break from school."

Everyone laughed.

"Why's that, Vi?" Grady asked. "Zayne Harrison still teasing you all the time?"

Her cheeks turned rosy. "Your turn, Grady."

"I'm thankful for my job with the vet and for this great family."

"I'm thankful," Deacon said, "for my new job as the vet at the stockyards."

Others continued until it was Boone's turn. "I'm thankful for a mule deer and my mulish woman who shot and dressed it expertly."

I laughed. Then I stopped.

"Wait, did you just call me mulish?"

He winked at me.

"I'm thankful for grizzly bears and bobcats."

Boone roared with laughter. Everyone else looked confused while I grinned at my husband. When he stopped laughing, he hugged me to his side. It was good to hear his laugh again.

"Remind me to tell you all the story about the bobcat," he said.

James frowned. When he glanced at my hand, his frown deepened, and he narrowed his eyes.

"I'm thankful for," James said, "new opportunities coming next year. That is if my surveyor finishes his job."

"James, enough." Will warned him.

Boone's smile faded, and he removed his arm from around me.

"Don't be cryptic, James," Boone said.

"What are you doing here?" he asked. "Shouldn't you be finishing up at Hell Canyon?"

"James, no business at the table," Hannah said firmly. "Not on Thanksgiving. We are glad Boone and his wife are home."

James practically spit out his food. "Wife? When did that happen?"

His tone was so acidic, I wanted to shrink under the table.

"We'll talk later," Boone said. His jaw twitched, and he straightened in his chair.

James let it go.

Ellie Mae's oldest son said something funny in his toddler language and broke the tension in the room.

"I'm sorry," I whispered to Boone.

He took my hand under the table and squeezed it. When I looked at him, he smiled.

The rest of the meal passed quickly. Boone seemed quiet

to me. Not like he was at camp. No stories told. No bright gleam in his eyes.

"We'll save pie for a little later," Hannah said. The women left the dishes and retired to the parlor. "Thanksgiving is the day the boys give us a break from the dishes."

While Will and Boone gathered up dishes from the table, James set his expensive suit jacket aside and rolled up his sleeves. Sam boiled some water, Deacon and Grady grabbed a towel each, and Preston left the house.

Once the table was cleared, Boone came over to check on me. "How's your shoulder? Do you want some willow bark tea?"

"I'm fine, thank you."

He went back to the kitchen to help James wash dishes.

"Boone is a new man," Ellie Mae said as she raised an eyebrow my direction.

"Is he?" I asked.

Hannah smiled. "He is certainly very attentive to you. I'm glad of it. Maybe more of what I tried to teach him sunk in than I thought."

"What was he like as a child?" I asked.

Hannah puffed her cheeks and let out a loud breath. "Difficult. Rambunctious. Wild."

I smiled. He was still all those things.

"I thought for sure he'd break his neck by the time he turned sixteen. When he started working with Mike Fremont as a surveyor, I was so relieved. It seemed to give him something to channel his energy."

"Surveying is not for the faint of heart," I said.

"Is it true that you worked with your father for years?" Vi asked. "How did you manage it?"

I leaned forward. "I love it. It's the perfect combination of everything I love doing and am good at. I get to be out in nature and appreciate God's creation for days on end. I draw maps and perform difficult calculations. It requires knowledge of flora, fauna, and geology."

As I described our job, my eyes darted toward the kitchen. Boone watched me.

"I hunt and fish. I hike and scale canyon walls. It's a never-ending adventure. I can't imagine life without being a survey-or."

When I glanced at Boone again, his shoulders slumped, and he turned his back to me. I wondered if I said something wrong.

"Surely you want to settle down and raise a family now that you're married," Hannah said.

My smile faded. It was the same as Papa's expectation. "Can't I do both? Papa did."

"Yes, but he's a man," Hannah said.

My heart raced as I suddenly realized she was right. My surveying days were over. I was not prepared to leave it all behind. I never wanted to. After all, I moved to Prescott so I could keep surveying. I slumped back against the chair as the conversation shifted. After another minute with my thoughts, I excused myself and went outside.

The cool breeze felt wonderful against my skin. I walked toward the lake and the short dock with a boat. As I sat on the dock, I lifted my face to the sun.

Please, Lord, let me continue doing what you created me to do. I can't imagine you made me this way without some purpose in mind.

As a shadow cast over me, I opened my eyes.

"Can I join you?" Boone asked.

I nodded.

He let out a long breath. "Jaclyn."

The breeze tickled a few hairs at the base of my neck.

"I must leave on Monday. I need to go to Hell Canyon to finish the job."

"I? Not we?"

He cleared his throat. "I."

I turned to face him as my eyes burned. "You're leaving without me."

"I'm sorry. I heard what you said to Mama. I..."

I twisted the gold band around on my finger.

"You are good at all those things. That makes it so much harder. But you have to stay here."

I frowned and pierced him with my eyes. "You decided."

"Jaclyn, you almost died."

"How many times have you almost died? Surveying takes incredible courage and tenacity which both you and I have in spades. We make a great team. You know we do."

"My decision is final."

Indignation burned in my chest. "Who says you get to decide?"

He tried to take my hands, but I folded my arms across my chest.

"I'm your husband. I'm the lead surveyor."

"Don't take this away from me. It flows through my veins. You know what that means. You feel it too."

"Please don't make this harder than it is. It pains me to do this. Even more after hearing your passion for the job." He clenched his jaw and shifted his position.

I stood and looked down at him. "I'd rather have a destroyed reputation than lose this."

Then I turned and stormed away.

"Jack!"

In that moment I hated him. I didn't marry him so he could take away my freedom and my job. As I set a quick pace on the path around the lake, I glanced over my shoulder. When I saw he didn't follow me, I slowed down.

I didn't leave California and my father to start a new job to end up in that position. Yet, that's exactly where I was.

When I entered the house, I caught Boone's gaze and glared at him with disgust. Then I stormed up the stairs to his room and slammed the door as hard as I could before I packed my clothes into my trunk. I was sliding it across the floor when he entered the room.

"What are you doing?"

"I'm leaving!"

"Please don't do this."

"Me? You did this."

I stuffed my papers into my saddlebags since he blocked my escape.

His voice softened. "Jaclyn."

I froze.

He came forward and gently clasped my arms. "Jaclyn."

The tears burned my eyes. Then the fury in me left as I collapsed against him and sobbed over the loss of my dreams.

CHAPTER 18

BOONE

All the times I had disappointed and frustrated my parents paled compared to the grief my decision invoked in Jaclyn. Even though I was her enemy at that moment, I held her close and comforted her, grateful that she let me. I was taking away everything she loved.

It was the right thing to do. She was still healing from the fall. She was my wife. It was my job to provide for her and protect her. Surveying was a dangerous job, and I couldn't let her do it. I almost caved when she reminded me of what a great team we were. We were a good team.

"Why? Can you at least explain it to me?" she pleaded.

I sighed.

"I must get the Hell Canyon survey done and map an alternate route before Christmas. Otherwise, James is going to fire me." It was a half-truth. I didn't believe James would follow through on the threat.

She pulled away from me. "Then you need me. There's no one better suited to the job. I know you. I know what you are looking for. No one else can do what I do."

She was right. But it didn't matter. I didn't marry her so

she could risk her life again. I married her to protect her.

"You and I have lived freer than most men and women. We've both been headstrong and blazed our own trail. We wrote adventure into the life we wanted to live."

I looked into her eyes. "But it's time that we both leave behind our childish ways and step into adulthood."

The words stabbed my chest. I imagined she felt the same.

She looked away.

Then I stood and left the room. I couldn't bear to see the hurt in her eyes any longer.

When I entered the parlor, Mama pulled me outside to the porch.

"I have a favor to ask."

I waited for her to continue.

"Preston's behavior troubles me and your father. I know you'll be a person short. Would you consider taking Preston?"

"Mama, his drinking puts us all at risk."

"Don't let him have anything."

I snorted. It's not like she let him drink. He obviously hid it well.

"Please. The trip will dry him out. He needs help."

At length, I finally agreed, against my better judgment. I knew Preston's presence would make the trip more difficult, and I doubted he would be much help.

The weekend did not get any better. Jaclyn barely said a word to me. Every night she cried herself to sleep, and I let her. Mama's gaze blamed me for my wife's sorrow. The days of storytelling and laughter felt like a distant memory. I didn't feel anything like the man I was before.

On Monday morning, I rose early. Mama packed some biscuits and bacon for me and the crew. When Preston didn't show up, I kicked his drunk body out of bed and got him on his horse.

After I saddled Outlaw, I looked back at the house. I stared for a good minute, hoping Jaclyn would at least say goodbye. When she didn't, I mounted my horse. With head held low, I turned him toward town.

By the time we arrived at the office, we still had a few hours to pack. I wasn't in the mood for chatter, so I said little as Dustin, Holt, and Charlie helped. Preston dozed in a chair nearby.

"You sure we gotta take him?" Holt asked.

"Maybe he'll be more useful when he sobers up," Charlie said.

"I miss Jack," Dustin said. "Can't she come?"

I cleared my throat as I shook my head.

"Boone?"

"Jaclyn?" I looked up and my heart warmed. She came to see me after all.

Then she ran toward me and threw her arms around my neck. "I'm so glad you haven't left yet."

I steered her to the back room, so we could have a private moment.

"What are you doing here?"

"I'm sorry," she said. "I didn't want you to leave thinking I was still mad at you. Give me some time, and I'll figure out how to get over it."

Relief filled me as I held her close.

"Boone, I love you. Please come back to me."

The breath left my lungs as she placed a hand on my neck and pulled my face closer. Then she stood on her tiptoes and pressed her lips against mine. Fire coursed through my veins, and I kissed her hard. Searching. Hoping her words were true. When I released her, she panted. Then she rested her head against my chest.

She loved me.

I knew I should say something, but the words stuck in my mouth.

She lifted her gaze to mine.

"I promise." It was all I could manage around the lump in my throat. She smiled before she released me.

"Boss!" Holt hollered from the office. "We need to get this stuff to the station."

"I have to go," I said as I ran my fingers down her neck.

"Go. I'll lock up."

I handed her the key. As I walked out the door, Charlie doused Preston with water.

"Time to go, kid."

I held back a chuckle glad that the crew would shape up Preston.

When I mounted Outlaw, Jaclyn stood in the doorway and waved to me with a smile on her face. I waved back. I appreciated how hard it was for her to come and I was glad she did.

———

We made it to Hell Canyon late Tuesday, despite Preston. He was sick most of the way to Ash Fork. More than once I threatened to leave him for the coyotes.

No sooner did we set up camp than Dustin lamented Jaclyn's absence.

"I miss Jack," Dustin said.

"Shut up, Dustin," Preston said. "You can't bring a woman to camp."

"But she was smart. She knew more than any of us except Boone."

Preston shoved Dustin. I stepped between them.

"Enough."

I thought it might take a miracle from on high for Preston to return to Colter Ranch in one piece. After two days, he was on my last nerve.

"Preston, go get firewood," I said.

Preston backed down and left to get the firewood. I took a deep breath and let it out slowly.

"Jack would have been significantly more useful than that kid," Holt muttered.

He was right. She would change her map from the last trip. As it was, that task fell to me and I was too busy dealing with Preston to sketch out anything very accurate.

The rest of us set up camp and waited for Preston to return with firewood. After an hour, he finally came back.

"Where have you been?" I asked.

He dropped the firewood in a pile. Charlie started building the fire before we lost all daylight.

Preston's eyes looked glassy. I grabbed him by his shirt collar and felt his vest. A flask. I took it and dumped it out. Then I shoved him to the ground and searched his gear. I found two more.

"Out here, if you aren't sober, you're gonna get one of us killed. I won't stand for this." I tossed the empty flasks at his feet.

He stood and charged at me, so I punched him in the gut. It wasn't hard enough to do any damage, but it knocked him off balance.

"Go set up your tent," I growled.

My eyes narrowed as he hesitated for a moment. Then he turned on his heel and set up his tent.

"Why is he here, again?" Holt asked.

"Mama." It was the only explanation I felt like giving.

Holt shook his head.

The next few days we finished up the survey of Hell Canyon. Preston refilled the water, hunted game, and cooked our meals. After a few days without alcohol, his sickness subsided, and he helped more.

During the rest of the expedition, I trained Dustin how to notate the readings from the transit. He asked good questions and he seemed to pick up things quickly. One day, he may become an assistant. But he was no Jaclyn.

CHAPTER 19

JACLYN

I woke late on the day Boone left for Hell Canyon. After I dressed, I ran downstairs.

"You missed him. He left a half hour ago," Hannah said.

"I need to talk to him."

"Hurry out to the barn. Ask Adam for a horse. He can help saddle it if needed."

Within a few minutes, I mounted a chestnut gelding and headed into town. I pulled to a stop in front of Boone's office. Relief filled me when I saw Outlaw waited for him at the hitching post. I tied the gelding next to him.

"Boone!" I yelled when I entered the office. My heart pounded as I searched for him.

"Jaclyn?"

Relief flooded me as I ran into his arms. I apologized and told him I loved him. I didn't mean to say the words yet.

Still, I hoped he would say that he loved me. When he didn't, I held back my disappointment until after he left.

Once he was out of sight, I brought my saddlebags into the office and sat down at his desk. He might not allow me to travel with him, but I could help.

The map I studied was from the first trip. I double checked the calculations and created a larger more permanent map from my notes. The report I wrote was about the conditions we found at the proposed bridge site. As I remembered the canyon, I drafted some calculations based on my estimates of the canyon depth. We could add to the report when Boone returned.

I locked the office up and headed back to the ranch, feeling restless just like the times between trips with Papa.

As I thought about Papa, I cringed. I decided I should write to him. Hannah gave me an envelope and some paper. Then I sat at the table while she prepared lunch.

> Dear Papa,
>
> I am writing to let you know that I arrived safely in Prescott. After a brief job as an assistant surveyor, I married the surveyor. His name is Boone Colter.
>
> With love,
>
> Jaclyn

I added our address at Colter Ranch. If someone was going into town soon, I would ask them to mail the letter. It seemed far too short, but I refused to tell him all the embarrassing details that led to my marriage. I hoped he would be happy since the outcome was what he desired.

After lunch, I asked Hannah if I could help with laundry, as my shoulder felt mostly better. She thanked me for the help.

The days blurred into a dreary week. Then something entirely unexpected happened.

A week after Boone left, Sam yelled my name from the front door. "There's a note for you from Boone."

My heart lodged in my throat as I stood and entered the dining room. Sam handed me the note.

"Need you for alt route. Bring horse and gear. Meet in Ash Fork on ninth."

My eyes went wide. "That's tomorrow!"

Need you.

Boone sent for me. Warmth filled my heart as I handed the note to Hannah. Then I ran upstairs to pack my trail clothes, notebook, and other supplies.

The next morning, Will picked out a horse for me to take. "This is Rosie. She's an excellent trail horse. You want a sidesaddle?"

"Heavens no." I laughed as I rubbed the rose-gray mare's face.

"Didn't think so."

"I made biscuits and bacon." Hannah said. "I know the boys love my biscuits."

"Thanks." I opened my saddlebags, and Hannah filled every spare inch with the food.

She gave me a hug before I mounted the horse. "You'll buy a hat before you go, right?"

I nodded.

"Be careful. And give Boone and Preston my love."

I thanked her and Will for all their help. Then I rode off to town. After a quick stop at the mercantile to purchase a new hat, I headed to the train station. James met me there and purchased the ticket for me and my horse. Boone must have sent him a note too.

As the passengers stared at my attire, I smiled. I didn't care. Boone sent for me.

When I arrived in Ash Fork, I looked around as I stepped off the train. Boone was easy to spot. Tall. Red beard. White cowboy hat. Broad shoulders.

My breath left as he waved at me. Within seconds he lifted me into his arms and twirled me around. He smelled like fresh soap. I breathed deeply of him as his arms loosened and he set my feet back on the ground.

I laughed. "What was that for?"

He pulled me close again and my heart raced at the feel of his solid frame.

"Miss me?" he asked.

"Of course. What made you change your mind?"

Instead of answering, he captured my lips with his. I wrapped my arms around his middle and returned his kiss as his hands explored my back. When he groaned, he slowed the kiss.

Once our lips parted, he whispered with a husky voice, "I missed you, wife."

"Mmm. I missed you, too."

Slowly he released me and laced his fingers with mine.

"Better go pick up your horse."

He laughed when he saw her. "Rosie. That's exactly the horse I would have picked for you. Adam did good."

"It was your father who picked her."

He grinned. "You hungry?"

"Starved."

He guided me to the dining room at the hotel. After we ordered, he started the conversation.

"I'm sorry I made you stay behind. I missed you the entire time. So did the boys. At least three times a day, Dustin mentioned your name."

"But?"

"But we also need your help. Preston has been more than a handful. I mapped nothing on the way down. I hope your original map will work for Hell Canyon."

I took a deep breath. "Thank you."

"How did you keep busy at the ranch?" he asked.

I scrunched up my nose. "Laundry. Cooking. Cleaning. It was so boring."

He chuckled that deep-bellied sound I loved. His blue eyes sparkled like they did before we married.

"Your mother sent biscuits and bacon."

"Hmm. Let's hide them from the others."

His smile faded as he took a bite of his dinner.

"I'm glad you came. I thought you might still be mad at me."

"Are you kidding? You said to bring a horse and gear. I knew what that meant."

I finished my meal and pushed the plate away.

"How is your shoulder?"

"All better."

"I thought we could meet up with the boys tomorrow. Stay the night here."

He wiggled his eyebrows as he paid for the meal.

My heart raced as he reached for my hand. Then he led me to our room.

As soon as the door was closed, he took off my hat and his. He set them on hooks on the wall. Then he placed one hand on my waist and the other on my neck.

His voice was husky when he spoke. "Jaclyn, I missed you so much."

As he pulled me into his arms, he crushed his mouth against mine and explored. Then he lodged one hand in my hair. The other caressed my back. My hands explored his back as I returned his kiss with equal intensity. He deepened the kiss stirring an ardent response from me.

Then he abruptly tore his lips away from mine, leaving me breathless.

"Jaclyn," he whispered. "Can we have our wedding

night now?"

I pushed back from him to see his face clearly. The desire in his eyes overwhelmed me. There was only one plausible answer I could give the man I loved.

"Yes."

Then, as he made me his wife, I gave him my entire heart. I was his, and he was mine.

CHAPTER 20

BOONE

The next morning when I woke up in Ash Fork with my wife by my side, my heart filled with joy. I loved her. Completely. If left up to me, I could not have selected someone better.

"Morning," I whispered as I ran a finger along her cheek.

She opened her eyes and stretched. I loved the way her mismatched eyes twinkled like the stars at night.

"I'm glad you sent for me. Even if you didn't take me with you, I'd wait for you here if it meant seeing you sooner when you returned."

I didn't want to leave her side or the bed. My heart longed for our lives to be as happy as that moment.

She smiled. "Don't we need to meet the boys?"

"Soon." I said before I kissed her, gently that time.

"Mmm. Are they really expecting us today? Couldn't we just stay here?" she asked.

I groaned. Then I forced myself away from my wife.

"Alright, fine," she teased. "I suppose we can go to work."

After we dressed, I returned the hotel key. Then we headed out.

"Mind if we ride fast? The earlier we arrive, the sooner we can pack up so we can continue tomorrow."

She smiled and kicked Rosie into a gallop. Outlaw snorted, and we followed.

When we arrived at camp, all the boys except Preston greeted Jaclyn.

"Thank the good Lord! Jack is back!" Dustin hollered.

"Jaclyn," I said.

"Jack is fine," she said. "My papa always called me Jack in the field."

Holt and Charlie greeted her with as much enthusiasm. Then She went to her saddlebags and opened them. "Now that I know you all really missed me, I have a surprise."

She tossed the container of biscuits and bacon to Holt. "From Hannah."

Holt opened the container and took a deep breath. "Think we have supper covered."

I looked around for Preston. He stood leaning against a nearby tree. He sucked in a long drag on a cigarette before he flicked it to the ground and snuffed it out.

"Preston!" Jaclyn called for him. "Your mama said she sends her love."

He nodded and took our horses to the corral before he rubbed them down.

I sighed. He was the moodiest person.

"Do you have your map?" I asked Jack.

She handed it over.

When I unrolled the larger paper, my eyebrow arched. "You copied it."

She winked at me as I laid out the map.

"I thought we would head out tomorrow. On the way

here, I assume this area," I pointed to the map, "could be the starting point into the canyon for the alternate route."

"Do you want to scout it out first? Or shall we bushwhack and measure?" she asked.

"We should scout around first. I'd like to hear your thoughts once you see the canyon floor in that area."

The five of us planned the next several days while Preston sulked. He seemed determined not to be an active participant in the expedition.

As the evening wore on, Jaclyn, and I excused ourselves from the rest of the group. I held the tent flap open for her.

"Seems small for two people," she said.

"You can snuggle close. I don't mind."

She laughed. "I didn't think you would."

I reclined on my pallet. Then I patted it. She laid down next to me.

"Boone?"

I rested my arm over her. "Hmm?"

"Is this a onetime trip? I don't want to get my hopes up that I'll continue to work with you."

I let out a slow breath. When I sent for her, I only thought about the immediate need. I needed her help on the alternate route. And I wanted her with me.

"I don't know. Can we figure it out as we go?"

"You tell me." She turned to face me. "You're the one who forbade me to come. I want to be here. Always."

Always. I wondered if that was true. When children came along, she might feel differently. I swallowed the lump in my throat. The thought of her in the field with child terrified me.

Then I stroked my hand over her long, silky hair.

"I don't want to make promises I can't keep."

She sighed. "Alright. I'll enjoy the moment."

"Oh, I forgot to tell you," she added, "I started on the report. It's back at the office, but we should be able to adjust it based on what you learned from last week."

I chuckled. "All that and laundry too."

She laughed. "I know. I'm amazing."

"That you are. Now go to sleep. We have an early morning."

"Hmm. Is sleep really what you want?"

I groaned. Not after that comment.

———

The next morning, we broke camp. To my surprise, Preston actually helped. He packed up the gear and secured it to the mules with none of us asking him to. It was nice. I only hoped it would last.

As we wound down into the canyon, Jack worked on a map. Rosie adjusted well to her unusual riding style as she worked.

Once we were at the bottom, I pulled Outlaw to a stop.

"There's another option for the train's descent since that was too steep for them."

"Show me," she said.

Holt and Charlie came with us as we headed northwest along the canyon floor.

"I thought that spot there."

Jack nodded. "I can see it. Want to take some readings?"

"Yeah, we can camp here and start clearing the brush for the line today."

We made good progress until the sun dipped low in the sky. The days grew shorter and colder since it was the second week of December. Less light during the day meant it would take us more days to complete the job.

After we finished measuring the entry point, we measured the canyon floor the next day. Then we broke camp and moved further into the canyon.

"Do you think the river floods during rainstorms?" Jack asked.

"Probably. Picture water as it runs off the side of the canyon. This might not be a viable alternate."

"That's what I was thinking."

The next morning, I rose early. Jaclyn slept, so I carefully slid out of the tent. I hiked up to the south rim of the canyon in the chilly winter air. Not a cloud dotted the sky as the sun rose in the east. Streaks of purples, blues, pinks, and oranges blazed across the sky. I breathed deeply of the crisp air as I sat down and hung my feet over the edge of the rim.

Lord, thank you for Jaclyn. Thank you for honoring our vows and softening her heart to love me so quickly. Thank you for making her a perfect helpmate. Show us how she can fulfill her dreams as a surveyor in our marriage.

As I watched our camp from my vantage point, Jaclyn emerged from our tent and looked around. She looked at the north rim and then the south. When she looked my direction, I waved to her. She waved back before she crossed the river by balancing on rocks. Then she headed up the same path I took to the south rim. A few minutes later, she joined me.

"I will never tire of mornings like this," she whispered. "There is nothing like being out in God's creation and watching it wake up under His magnificently painted sky."

I placed my arm around her and drew her to my side. We sat there with our feet dangling over the edge until the rest of the camp woke. Then, reluctantly I led her back down to the river bottom.

After a few more days, we were ready to make a recommendation. It took us a week to make it back to Ash Fork since we stopped for more measurements. We explored part of the area to the west. Nothing presented an obvious solution. I figured we would have to explore even further west on another trip if James wanted to pay for it.

By the time we arrived in Ash Fork, it was late in the day, so we stayed overnight. Jaclyn and I spent the night in the hotel. I think Preston disappeared to a saloon. The crew stayed with the horses and camped just outside of town.

When we retired to our room, Jaclyn's mood turned solemn, and I wondered why.

CHAPTER 21

JACLYN

The morning after we arrived back in Ash Fork, I sat across from Boone in the hotel dining room for breakfast. Too many things were on my mind. I wasn't sure if he loved me or not. We were intimate several times since I arrived two weeks ago. Even though he spoke to me tenderly and affectionately, I didn't know if that meant he loved me. It was over two weeks since I hastily declared my love for him. I wanted to hear that he loved me too. I held back a groan. That was what happened when one rushed into a marriage before courting.

I sighed.

"Jaclyn?" Boone asked. "What's on your mind?"

Shaking my head, I took a bite of my breakfast. I didn't want to fish for the words from him. I wanted him to say he loved me of his own volition without me coaxing them out of him. It was the only way I could trust his sincerity.

He took my hand. "I know you're sad about the end of the trip."

I nodded. That was part of my mood.

"We'll figure it out."

As I waited for him to pay for the meal, I drank a swig of coffee. Then I stood and followed him to the room.

"Did you bring a dress for the trip home?"

"No," I said brusquely. "Why would I need a dress?"

His eyes went wide, and he said nothing else as I packed my saddlebag. Then we checked out and headed to the camp.

When we arrived, no one knew Preston's whereabouts. While the rest of us checked in at the train station, Boone tried to find him. A few minutes after the inbound train whistle sounded, he appeared without Preston.

"I guess he'll find his own way home."

He left money and a note with the train stationmaster to send Preston back to Prescott if he showed up.

We boarded the train and headed toward Seligman, then home to Prescott.

As I stared out the window, a tear slid down my cheek. I'd miss surveying. It was my life for six years, and I did not want it to end. Perhaps Boone would let me help in the office. I really wanted to.

He reached over and rubbed the base of my neck. "I wish you would tell me what is on your mind."

I turned to look at him, and the tears fell. "I don't want to give up my career."

His lips formed a thin line. A frown flitted away. "I know."

That was all he said. No promises. No hope.

As my gaze focused on the scenery that blurred by, I pulled away from him. I was created to be an assistant surveyor. But I was also a wife. One day I would be a mother.

Why couldn't I be all three? Why did I have to give up my career?

As the sway of the train lulled me to sleep, I leaned

against Boone and closed my eyes.

"Jaclyn." Boone nudged me. "Wake up."

I opened my eyes and stretched as the train slowed and stopped in Prescott. I stepped down from the train and headed toward the stock car. Boone and the crew followed behind me. We each retrieved our mounts. Then we headed back to the office. Boone rented a wagon and picked up the rest of our gear from the train station.

After I dropped my stuff in the office, I went out back to pump some water to freshen up. When I returned to the main room of the office, I heard my name. I walked toward the front and stopped short at the sight of my father. My heart dropped to the floor.

"Papa," I said cautiously.

"Jaclyn." His terse greeting told me I was in a great deal of trouble. "I received your letter."

I nodded. "How long have you been in town?"

"Close to two weeks."

I hugged him stiffly. "I'm glad to see you."

"I'm glad you're safe. What's this business about a marriage?"

Holt, Charlie, and Dustin scurried out of the building with a muffled promise to see us after Christmas.

"Like I said in my letter, I'm married to Boone Colter."

Papa frowned. "You need to get it annulled."

Boone entered the office as Papa said the words. He frowned at me.

"Papa, this is my husband, Boone."

"Sir." Boone extended his hand in greeting. Papa looked at it for several seconds before he shook it.

"This is my father, Silas Bennett."

"Pleased to meet you," Boone added and flashed one of his charming grins.

"We will talk about this later," Papa said.

"Have you been out to the ranch?" I asked.

"It was the only address I had for you. Sam brought me in to show me your office and James said he expected you back before Christmas."

"I'm sorry you've been waiting so long." The awkwardness made my skin crawl. I sighed.

"Come back with us," Boone said. "Spend Christmas with my family at the ranch."

Papa's eyes narrowed, and he lifted his chin as he measured Boone.

"Please, Papa."

"Alright."

"Did my family loan you a horse?" Boone asked.

"Yes. They have been very gracious."

My stomach plummeted to my knees as I realized he likely spent the better part of two weeks at the ranch. I hoped Will and Hannah said things to help ease his anger and shock.

"We'll be ready to head back in about a half hour," Boone said. "Please make yourself at home."

We unpacked our gear. As I cleaned the transit, Papa stood and helped.

"Is this the '74 model?" he asked.

I let out a quiet breath. "Yes. Its siting telescope can handle greater distances. It held up well over some rugged country."

Papa nodded as he used a fine brush to clear the dust and dirt from the mechanics of it. Then he rubbed a cloth over it to polish the brass pieces.

While he remained distracted, I stepped away and unpacked my notes, map, and other gear.

"Is this the report you started?" Boone asked as he picked

it up from his desk.

"Yes."

He flipped through several pages. "This is good. This will save us time after Christmas."

"Should we plan to work on the report at the ranch?" I asked.

"No. Let's leave everything here. We'll come into town after the weekend. Then we'll work on getting the final report ready for James."

Papa let out a satisfied sigh as he finished cleaning the transit. Then he stepped back and smiled at his handiwork.

"I heard him," Boone whispered, "about an annulment."

"It's not an option," I said.

When I glanced up at Boone, he did not look convinced. Besides the fact that we consummated our marriage, I also wouldn't consider it because I loved him.

"He'll come around," I said. "He wanted me to settle down and get married. It just happened differently than what he expected. He likes to be in control. I'm sure this shocked him."

I squeezed Boone's hand.

We finished at the office and mounted our horses. Papa rode beside me, and Boone followed behind us.

"Jaclyn, I was quite shocked to find you gone when I returned from my trip."

"I know. I'm sorry, Papa. When I moved to take the position with Boone, I wanted to keep my job so desperately I didn't think about the consequences."

I glanced back at Boone. What a trail of damage it was. My actions forced him into a marriage he never wanted. I appreciated he tried to make it as good as possible. But that did not absolve me of my sins.

"I'm sorry that I hurt you, Papa."

He sighed heavily. Then he looked at me. "I'm relieved to see you. I imagined the worst, despite Will and Hannah's assurances that you were safe."

"Where have you been staying?" I asked.

"Hannah set up Preston's room for me. She said she would send him to the bunkhouse when he returns."

I nodded. Who knew when that would be. I imagined Boone dreaded seeing his mother since we came back without him.

Despite my anxiety, I was glad Papa would spend Christmas with us. I missed him more than I realized.

When we arrived back at the ranch, it was early afternoon. Hannah made us some sandwiches.

Then she warmed water for baths and hung a sheet in the kitchen to give us privacy. I bathed first. It felt so good to scrub the dirt and grime from my hair. When I finished Boone bathed. Then he dumped out the dirty water.

After we took our things upstairs, I changed out of my robe and into one of my work dresses. Then I braided my hair even though it was still damp. Boone donned some clean trousers and a clean cotton shirt.

It was good to be home.

CHAPTER 22

BOONE

"Where is Preston?" Mama grilled me as soon as I came down from upstairs.

I sighed heavily. "Honestly, I don't know. The moment we arrived back in Ash Fork, he headed straight for the saloon."

"I asked you to help him sober up."

"And he was for two weeks."

Mama frowned at me.

"Look, he is his own man. I left a note and a ticket for him at the train station. When he's ready to come home, he can."

"He could be dead!"

I let out a loud breath. "He's not dead. Not yet. He might be when Papa gets a hold of him."

Mama grumbled under her breath.

To work through the disturbing turn of events, I walked around the lake. My heart nearly broke in two when I heard Jaclyn's father suggest an annulment. I loved her. She was no longer his responsibility since she was my wife now.

I stuffed my hands in my pockets as I walked, and I

COLTER SONS BOOK 2

shook my head. Mama was being unreasonable. Silas wanted to take Jaclyn away. James was running out of patience with me. And my wife distanced herself from me. I couldn't fix any of it.

I ran a hand through my hair as I picked up my pace around the lake until my heart throbbed. Blood pumping through my veins usually soothed me, but not then.

In a few months, my life turned upside down. I owned a business, managed a crew, and gained a wife. My mama was disappointed because I did not haul my mercurial brother back home. Silas wanted a different son-in-law. And my wife would not talk to me.

Deep down, I wanted to jump on Outlaw's back and ride until sunset. I shook my head. That would solve nothing.

"Boone!" Papa called to me as I rounded the last curve of the lake toward the ranch house.

"Papa."

"I heard Preston did not come back."

"No, sir."

He sighed heavily. "It's not your fault. I know Hannah is upset, but Preston chooses a dark path, despite our best efforts to help him. She's just worried about him."

"As am I. But there's only so much I can do. He was difficult to work with."

"I can imagine." Papa squeezed my shoulder. "Thank you for trying."

I nodded.

"I see you met Jaclyn's father."

"Barely. But yes." I turned to face him. "He wants her to annul our marriage."

Papa rubbed a hand over his face. "I thought he might."

"It's not possible. We… It's not possible."

Papa's mouth quirked up in a half-smile. "Good for you."

"I'm afraid she might want the same as her father," I admitted. "It would be her word against mine."

Papa stopped walking. "Then fight for your wife."

I wanted to ask him how, but the words died on the tip of my tongue.

Papa sighed. "I know you want to do the right thing. It's one of your finer qualities. Don't let Silas bully you into something you don't want. Talk to Jaclyn. She might feel differently than what you think."

"She told me she loves me," I whispered.

"What did you say in response?"

"Nothing. I was leaving on the trip."

Papa shook his head. "Son, how do you feel about her?"

I kicked at a rock in the dirt. "I love her."

Papa slapped me on the back. "Then you better tell her that. Sooner rather than later. A woman doesn't like to guess how you feel. She will need to hear the words from you."

I shook my head. "I'm terrible at this."

His laughter floated on the air. "Time and communication are the only two things that will change that."

"I miss laughing," I said.

"You started a new business and had a shotgun wedding all at the same time. As Solomon said, there is 'a season for every activity under the heavens. A time to weep and a time to laugh. A time to tear and a time to mend. A time for love and a time to hate.' You'll laugh again soon."

"I suppose I need to mend some things with Jaclyn and her father."

"And love. Love them both."

I nodded and followed Papa into the house. For the first time in my life, he spoke to me man to man, sharing wisdom of one who lived in a marriage for a long time. His relationship with Mama was good. I suppose I thought it was easy because it appeared to us that it was. Perhaps even their marriage endured some difficult times.

When we entered the house, I found Jaclyn and her father in the parlor. I took a seat next to her.

"I hope my family made you feel welcome in our absence," I said to Silas.

"Oh, yes. Your parents were very welcoming. They tried to reassure me that Jaclyn was fine and in good hands."

"I apologize I did not ask for Jaclyn's hand properly."

Silas cleared his throat. "From what Jaclyn explained, there wasn't much time for that."

"I hope that in time you can forgive me."

"Boone, don't take the blame for this," Jaclyn said. "You've been more than honorable trying to fix my mistake."

She reached over and squeezed my hand. I smiled at her.

"I am the one to blame for this mess. I never considered what would happen if I was caught, so I am asking for forgiveness from both of you."

A tear slid down her cheek, and she wiped it away.

I winked at her. "You are forgiven."

I wanted to say more. But it wasn't the right time to declare my love for her or my gratitude that she was my wife.

"Supper is ready!" Mama called.

I stood and pulled Jaclyn close for a quick hug. Then I led her to the table and held out a chair for her. Silas sat across from me as Sam and his family entered the house and took their seats.

"Where's Preston?" Deacon asked.

"He stayed behind in Ash Fork," Papa said. His stare let Deacon know to drop the conversation.

Silas seemed comfortable with the sizeable crowd at supper. He smiled at Ellie Mae's baby several times. When Brody fussed, Silas surprised both me and Jaclyn as he offered to hold the baby for a while.

"I've never seen Papa hold a baby," Jaclyn said.

Silas smiled at her. "I used to hold you all the time when you were a baby. You were the cutest baby, no offense Ellie Mae."

Ellie Mae laughed. "None taken. I'm certain every father feels the same about their little girls."

Papa smiled. "Vi was the cutest of you."

"Thanks, Papa," Vi said.

"Better looking than me?" I teased.

Everyone laughed, including me.

When Brody calmed, Silas placed him in the bassinet in the parlor. Then he took his seat again.

"Jaclyn mentioned you just started your own surveying business. How is that going?" he asked.

"So far, it's going well. Our client has lined up more work for us."

"Yes, Jaclyn mentioned it's another railroad."

I nodded. "Though that is not common knowledge."

"Understood. She said you have a small crew."

"It's the same size as what we used for surveying the mines. But we need to expand. I could see us with a few crews, especially if the railroad moves forward with construction next year. The line will run from Ash Fork all the way to Phoenix."

"Sounds like you could use some help."

I nodded. "Do you have someone in mind?"

"My crew is between jobs at the moment. We could commit to a few months' work starting in January."

"How big is your crew?" I asked and then took a swig of

my water.

"Ten men, a cook, a laundress, and a wrangler."

I nearly spit out my water. I coughed and Jaclyn patted my back.

"I have two young men that I've been mentoring to become assistant surveyors. I was going to reply to your letter and send you one of them, but it seems Jaclyn beat me to it."

He winked at her.

"Our next goal is to scout out an alternate route from Ash Fork to Prescott. The Hell Canyon route is probably not going to happen. So, we'll have to figure out a reasonable path through the mountains."

"Next time we're in town, I can wire them to be here the first week of January."

"That sounds good. We can settle the details tomorrow."

He agreed, and I wondered what changed his mind about me. Certainly, he would not be offering help if he planned to take Jaclyn back to California with him.

The rest of the evening passed quickly. Silas and I spoke in more detail about the plan before Jaclyn and I retired to our room.

As I climbed into bed next to her, I rolled onto my side and snuggled against her back. I rubbed my hand on her arm and kissed her shoulder.

"I love you, Jaclyn."

Soft breathing was the only response. She fell asleep before she heard the words.

I sighed and rolled onto my back. I would try again in the morning.

CHAPTER 23

JACLYN

The next morning, I woke to the feeling of being watched. Boone laid on his side with his head propped on one hand. He studied me as my eyes opened and connected with his.

"Morning," he whispered as he rubbed a hand along my arm.

"Morning." I smiled at him.

"Miss seeing that."

My smile stretched bigger.

"You fell asleep pretty fast last night."

"I was exhausted."

He trailed a finger along my jawline. "You missed a very important conversation."

The look in his eyes stole my breath away. "Did I?"

"Yes. I told you I love you, Jaclyn. I do. I love you and I'm grateful that you are my wife."

I blinked several times as my eyes burned. "You love me?"

He pulled me closer. "Very much."

"But—"

He placed a finger on my lips.

"I love your eyes. One amber, one green. Mysterious. Intriguing."

Heat warmed my cheeks. "Go on."

"I love your personality, your intelligence. You are by far the smartest woman I've met. You are kind and funny. When we are in the field, you like to help other people."

I let out a slow breath.

"And for some strange reason, you love me. So, dear wife, I love you. I won't let you go."

"So, you don't want rid of me?" I asked. I closed my eyes as I was afraid of what his answer might be.

"Never."

Then he captured my lips with his. I gave into his kiss for a moment before I pushed back slightly.

"Are you sure?"

He laughed. "Positive. God knew what He was doing when He allowed our paths to cross. He knew I would be thickheaded and need a woman like you. No, not like you. He knew I need you, Jaclyn. I thank Him for you."

"Even though you felt compelled to marry me?"

"I think it might have been the only way to get my attention. It doesn't matter. It's how we met and married. That part of our past does not have to define our future. I love you. You love me. Good marriages have been built on far less."

I let his words sink into my heart. He loved me. He thanked God for... For me. I didn't deserve him. But he was mine. My husband.

As I leaned forward and kissed him, he kissed me back with a tender love that slowly heated to the love that a husband expresses for his wife.

When I was ready to leave the embrace of my beloved, I

swung my legs over the side of the bed and stood. He rolled out of bed on his side.

"I smell bacon," he said. "We better hurry. I think we're late for breakfast."

I giggled. "Hopefully your mother will forgive us this once."

I hurriedly dressed and fixed my hair. He waited for me and took my hand in his as we ran down the stairs.

When we entered the dining room, all eyes turned our way in mid-bite.

"Good morning, family!" Boone greeted them loudly.

"Boone is back," Deacon muttered under his breath.

"You're late," Hannah said, but her smile held no scolding.

Boone held a chair out for me. I sat, and he sat next to me.

Everyone returned to their meal and discussed plans for Christmas Eve day.

"I thought we should go into town to get some gifts for the family," Boone said.

"And each other?"

He winked. "Of course."

In the end, the entire family and Papa went to town. Boone and I rode our horses to free up room in the wagon for Sam's wife and children.

Once we arrived in town, we split up. I went to the mercantile. I wasn't sure where Boone went, but he said he would meet me at the mercantile after he went somewhere else first.

I noticed while we were out surveying that his work gloves were falling apart, so I went to the aisle with leather gloves. I picked out a nice brown pair. Then I studied them for a minute to figure out if they were large enough. I held them up to my hands and tried to picture his hand when he held mine. My hand looked so small compared to the glove.

"That size should work for Boone," Hannah said as she came up next to me.

I smiled and thanked her. Then I looked around and picked out something for Papa. I asked the clerk to wrap both items to keep the surprise.

By the time Boone joined me, I picked out a few items for his parents, Ellie Mae, and Vi. He liked what I selected. Then he added some gifts for his brothers and nephews.

When we stepped outside, the temperature was colder than before. Heavy clouds rolled in.

"We might have a white Christmas this year," Boone said as he helped me carry our purchases to the wagon. "It's been years since it snowed." His eyes lit with excitement.

"I don't think we've ever had snow on Christmas in Sacramento."

Papa overheard our conversation. "Not on Christmas. A few years ago, we got that freak snowstorm right after New Year's."

"I remember. We tried to make snowballs, but that didn't really work."

The train whistle blew about the time we were ready to return home.

"I'm going to wait to see if Preston is on the train," Boone said. "Just ask Deacon or Grady to carry our things in when you get home."

I kissed him on the cheek and mounted my horse.

Papa rode next to me on the way home.

"I'm sorry I suggested an annulment yesterday," he said. "It's clear that you are a good match."

I quirked an eyebrow. "You really believe that?"

He nodded. "I don't know how the two of you ended up

together. From everything I've seen, I'm convinced he will move heaven and earth for you if needed."

I smiled as I adjusted my coat against the whipping cold wind.

"Now, if you give me some grandchildren, I wouldn't mind."

"Papa!"

He chuckled. I watched as the stress of the last few weeks faded from his features.

"After Christmas, do you think you'll move into town?"

"We haven't discussed it. Honestly, everything about our relationship seems backwards and upside down. As soon as we returned from our first trip, he had to turn around and head out again. I stayed behind for the first week, but I still lived at the ranch."

"You should discuss it. Even though his family is wonderful, you will need your own place and some privacy. Plus, if my crew and I are going to help Boone in January, it would be nice to know you'll be in town waiting for us."

I frowned. "I want to go with him."

"The sooner you let that go, the happier you will be."

I bit the inside of my cheek. I was not ready to give up surveying.

"Boone has said nothing." I lifted my chin.

"Jaclyn." Papa's voice warned. "Do nothing foolish."

"I won't." My shoulders sagged in defeat.

I knew Papa tried to prepare me for the reality of my new life. I wanted to be involved. Even if it meant working in the office instead of going into the field. I was good at my job, and it seemed like such a waste of my skills and talents to only take care of a home. I was capable of so much more.

Sometimes, I felt like my ambition was a curse. If I were

a man, they would consider it an asset or an edge. But as a woman, the opportunity I wanted was not available to me.

When we arrived back at the ranch, snow fell. I hoped Boone would not delay his trip home. I hated the thought of him being stuck out in the snow.

CHAPTER 24

BOONE

The train pulled into the station as I tied Outlaw to the hitching post out front. I stepped onto the platform and scanned the faces of the crowd as they exited the train. Then I saw a conductor with his arm around a young man. I closed my eyes. Preston was so drunk he could not stand on his own two feet.

I approached the conductor. "Did he board his horse on the train?"

"I'm not sure. Do you know what it looks like?"

I nodded.

"Go on back. If you spot it, take it."

"Thank you," I said as I looped my arm around Preston's side.

He leaned up against me so heavily that I dragged him as I walked. When we came to a bench, I slid him onto it.

"Stay put."

He waved his arm limply.

Then he heaved when I walked away. I shook my head. I did not understand why he did that to himself. He grew up in the same house as me. Same parents. He lived a good life. Yet, he preferred to drown his emotions with liquor.

When I approached the stock car, I quickly spotted his liver chestnut stallion, Ranger. Thankfully, Ranger recognized me and snorted. I led him over to where I deposited Preston.

He passed out, so I slung his lax body over his saddle on his stomach as snow fell. Then I led Ranger out of the train station. I held his reins as I mounted Outlaw. Then we walked a painfully slow pace back to the ranch. A few times, I stopped to readjust Preston, so he didn't slide off the horse and into the accumulating snow.

At last, we arrived home. Deacon waited for us at the barn.

"He's out cold," I said.

Deacon sighed. "Mama is fretting like crazy."

"Where are we going to put him? Jaclyn's father is in his room."

"We can put him in with me and Grady. He can sleep on the floor."

"Probably will need a bucket handy. Might keep you up at night."

Deacon quirked a half-smile. "Thankfully, I have the next few days off, with it being Christmas."

I dismounted. Deacon offered to care for the horses and asked me to send Grady out.

Then I carried Preston to the house. Grady opened the door, already wearing his coat. He headed out to the barn. Sometimes I thought he and Deacon read each other's thoughts with the way they anticipated each other's actions.

"Preston!" Mama called out as soon as she saw him.

"I'm gonna take him up to Deacon's room."

She objected but followed me upstairs. When I laid him on the floor, she wouldn't let me.

"Put him in Deacon's bed."

I frowned but did what she asked.

As soon as he was out of my arms, she checked him from head to toe for injuries. Not once, but twice. I rolled my eyes.

After I went downstairs, I grabbed an extra bucket. Then I took it outside and filled it with water as the snow fell faster. Once I took the full bucket upstairs, I poured some of the clean water in the washbasin. I left some water in the bottom to mask the odor when he threw up again. I did not envy Deacon and Grady.

Mama thanked me. She dipped a cloth in the water and wiped the dirt from his face.

When I went downstairs, Papa pulled me aside for an update. I told him what little I knew. Then I sat in the parlor by the fire to warm up. I patted my pocket to make sure Jaclyn's gift was still there.

"I thought I heard you come in." Jaclyn entered the parlor. "Was Preston with you?"

"Yes. About in the shape that I thought."

She sighed. "Do you want some coffee? Papa? Will?"

We all agreed. Jaclyn set a pot on the stove in the kitchen. I stood to help her.

When she turned her back to me, I pulled her into my arms and rested my chin on her head. She leaned back against me. I swayed as if I heard music in my mind. We stayed like that until the coffee finished brewing. Then I slowly released her.

She smiled as she poured the coffee. "I could get used to you doing things like that."

"Me too."

I took two of the cups and handed one to my papa. Then I sat on the couch and patted the spot next to me.

Jaclyn gave her papa one mug and sat beside me.

Deacon and Grady entered the house.

"There's some fresh coffee on the stove," she told them, but remained seated.

"The snow is really coming down." Grady crossed the room and sat on the floor in front of the fire. He held his coffee in both hands.

"I don't think Ellie Mae and Sam will venture over in this weather for supper," Deacon said as he sat next to Grady.

They asked about Preston. I told them Mama was upstairs fussing over him.

When Mama still did not come downstairs, Jaclyn asked if she should start supper.

"That would be a big help to Mama," I said.

She stood and took care of it. Vi joined her.

"Are you going to move?" Deacon asked me.

Papa nodded his agreement.

"I guess so." With everything else on my plate, I forgot about it. "I suppose this weekend, if the weather clears, we'll look for a place in town."

"If you need some help," Papa said, "let me know."

I thanked him.

"Will!"

The panic in Mama's voice caused me to jump to my feet. I was the first up the stairs.

"What is it?"

Preston convulsed.

"Hold him."

I did as she asked.

Papa entered the room.

"Bring my bag," Mama said.

Papa ran back downstairs.

"Sit him up," she said, "so he can breathe easier."

I sat next to him and held him upright.

Papa returned with Mama's medical bag as Preston stopped convulsing.

"The ipecac."

Papa handed it to her.

She poured some onto a spoon. "Hold his mouth open."

I did so.

She tipped the spoon into his mouth. "Swallow for me, Preston."

To my surprise, he did.

Papa sat on his other side.

When Preston gagged, Mama held the bucket up to him.

"Come on, son. You gotta get it out of your system," Papa said.

"Anything we can do?" Deacon asked from the doorway.

"Get another bucket ready," Papa said.

Deacon came back with another bucket as Preston wretched. Papa swapped out the buckets. Then Deacon cleaned the used one and brought it back.

Tears streamed down Mama's face, but she stayed calm. When it looked like my job was done, I stood. She took my place and cooed calming words to him.

"I don't understand," Mama said what we all thought.

"You boys go on down for supper," Papa said.

"Yes, sir."

I closed the door behind us.

As I stepped off the last stair, Vi asked, "Is he going to die?"

"Not under Mama's care," I replied.

"'Cause there was this boy at school. His papa drank

himself to death. Is that what Preston did?"

Deacon hugged her to his side. "Vi, he'll be fine. Don't worry."

Once Vi calmed down, she helped Jaclyn set the food out. I blessed the meal, which felt completely foreign to me. Papa always did that.

Grady and Deacon tried to take everyone's minds off what was going on upstairs as we ate. Vi glanced over her shoulder many times. Silas and Jaclyn looked somber. I felt like they looked.

Vi and Jaclyn left a plate for Mama and Papa on the stove. Then they cleaned up the kitchen.

It was another hour before they came downstairs. Deep lines etched in Papa's forehead, and Mama looked weary. Deacon and Grady went upstairs to keep an eye on Preston as Papa tried to convince Mama to eat.

My heart hurt for my parents.

———

Throughout Christmas Eve, I woke to the sounds of my parents helping Preston. I learned the next morning that Deacon and Grady stayed in my parents' room while my parents sat with Preston in Deacon and Grady's room.

Christmas morning dawned. Jaclyn and Vi made break-fast for us. Then Jaclyn found the ham and started it in the oven.

When Mama and Papa joined the family later in the morning, they tried to force a cheerful mood for the rest of us. While we exchanged gifts, Deacon volunteered to sit with Preston.

Jaclyn started by giving Silas a gift from both of us. That was nice of her.

After we exchanged a few other gifts, I approached Jaclyn and handed her my gift as I held my breath while she opened it. Her different colored eyes sparkled when she lifted the gold compass broach from the paper. She laughed.

"Oh, Boone, this is perfect." She hugged me.

I held her close and whispered, "It's so you'll remember that I will always find my way back to you."

She kissed my cheek. Then she handed me her gift.

I unwrapped it. Then I grinned. "I take it you noticed my old gloves needed replaced."

She nodded as I tried them on. They fit perfectly. I hugged her close.

The family's mood lifted some throughout the afternoon, especially when Preston improved. We set his and Deacon's gifts aside, along with the gifts for Sam's family.

On Sunday morning, the weather lifted, and we all made it to church, including a pale-looking Preston. After church, we enjoyed a normal Sunday supper and finished exchanging gifts with those who missed Christmas Day.

I smiled as I watched Jaclyn interact with my family. She belonged there. With me and with my family.

CHAPTER 25

JACLYN

Over the weekend, the snow melted, and the ground dried out. By the time Boone and I headed to town Monday morning, the roads cleared.

We dropped off our saddlebags at the office. Then Boone took the horses to the livery while I met with a real estate agent. By the time Boone joined me at the real estate agent's office, I picked out a few houses to look at.

Boone ruled out the first without seeing it. He thought it was too expensive. I sighed. It was my favorite.

We looked at two houses. In the end we, or more accurately, Boone chose the smaller, cheaper two-bedroom home a few blocks from the office. I was not fond of the house. Even though it felt very cramped to me, I stuffed down my complaints as we walked to the office.

Once we arrived at the office, Boone sat on one side of the desk. I sat next to him with my map spread out on top of the desk. He flipped through his notes, and we discussed what to include in the report. By the time we were ready to write the report, it was early afternoon.

"When are we moving into the house?" I asked.

"Today."

I blinked. "Don't you think we need a bed and some furniture?"

He ran a hand through his hair. "Fine, let's go find some-thing."

We went to one of the furniture shops in town and picked out the cheapest bed, cheapest table and two chairs. That was it. Nothing for the living room. No dresser or nightstands. No place for a washbasin. I bit back my frustration.

He left me at the house and asked his cousin, Eddie, to help deliver the furniture. Once they were done, he sat down at the table.

"Boone, I don't mean to be difficult. But how am I supposed to cook or clean? We don't have any pots and pans or plates or silverware. Or linens for the bed. Or, well, anything."

"We need to watch our finances," he said. "The railroad has not paid us for the Hell Canyon job and my reserves are shrinking fast."

"But didn't your parents say they would help?"

"I'm not taking money from them."

I flopped down onto the other chair at the table. "How do you propose we eat?"

"Go to the mercantile and purchase only what we need for supper tonight. I'll bring the rest of our things from the ranch tomorrow. Maybe Mama has some old dishes we can borrow."

"I have some money left," I volunteered. "Papa paid me for the jobs I did with him. I can wire for the rest tomorrow."

He frowned and ran a hand through his hair again.

"Fine."

I hurried out the door to get the necessities before he changed his mind. He was not happy. He did not like using money I earned, and I didn't understand why. We were married.

Since I bought more than I could carry home, I bribed a young lad to bring the rest for a quarter. Boone didn't need to know.

Except he was home when I returned.

"How much did you spend?"

"I covered it myself. I bought food for the week and just one pan and a coffeepot, two plates and silverware, two mugs. A dish towel. Practically nothing, alright."

He frowned again.

I was hungry, so I started dinner while he went out back and chopped some wood. It felt like I did something wrong, but I didn't know what.

While I cooked supper, he started a fire in the fireplace. He opened the door to our bedroom and closed off the second bedroom. I set out our meager place settings and our supper. We sat in silence and ate.

Inwardly, I prayed he would not be too proud to accept some things from Hannah. At bedtime, I brought my coat with me since we still had no linens, blankets, or pillows for the bed. I slept in my dress and coat with my arm under my head. He did the same. When I shivered, he scooted closer and wrapped one arm around me.

A tear slid down my cheek. I'd rather be camping in the wilderness than live like paupers in town.

The next morning, I woke to a frigid house. I wore my coat as I started the stove. Then I fried some eggs and bacon. Breakfast was lighter than what Hannah served, but I needed to ration what I purchased. I set the coffeepot on to boil.

"Morning," I greeted Boone as he entered the main room of the house.

He nodded. Then he went outside and brought in a stack of wood for the fireplace.

When he sat down, I set a plate in front of him. He frowned so often I expected a frown for everything I did.

"That's it?"

I raised my chin. "Yes."

He finished in roughly five bites. Then he stormed out of the house without a word.

After I washed the dishes, I walked to the office and started a fire in the stove there. I sat down at the desk and worked on the survey report of Hell Canyon and the alternate route.

Around eleven, he finally joined me. He handed me a sandwich before he took a seat at the desk.

"Mama sent this in with me."

I thanked him and took the sandwich.

"She also gave us some bedding, blankets, pillows, and some things for the kitchen."

"That was kind of her."

"Your father rode in and booked a room at the boarding-house. He wants to store some things in our spare room when we leave for the Rock Butte survey."

"Of course," I said.

"I'm sorry," he murmured as he looked at the corner of the room.

"For?"

"I'm sorry I am so unprepared to give you a suitable home." His gaze returned to his sandwich.

I sighed. "It's not like you were expecting to get married this year."

He snorted. "No. I wasn't. And I'm not trying to be

stingy. Just careful. The business is eating into more of my savings than I expected. It wasn't a problem until now. I didn't plan for rent and horse boarding fees."

"Well, the report is progressing nicely. We can send it to James tomorrow and collect payment from him."

Boone picked up the report and started reading it while he ate his sandwich. He flipped through his notes.

After several hours, he finally said, "I think you covered what I would have. We just need to complete the maps and get Holt's geological report added. I'll send a message to him to come in tomorrow."

I stood and stretched. "Can we call it a day?"

He stood and held my coat for me. Then he shrugged his coat on and we walked home.

When he opened the door, my jaw dropped. He frowned.

"What's all this?" he asked me.

"That was my question for you."

There was a couch and a few chairs, end tables, oil lamps, and throws in the living area. Four more chairs graced the table. I walked over to the cupboards and opened them. Fully stocked with food, dishes, pans, and more.

I placed my coat on a hook by the door before I hurried into the bedroom. Two nightstands, a dresser, washbasin, and bedding on the bed. I blinked a few times to make sure it was real.

When I went back to the table, Boone held a note. "It's from our parents."

He handed it to me. "Boone, Jaclyn, Every married couple needs help. This is from your Papa, Silas, and me. We hope our gift will make you feel more comfortable as you start your new life together. Love, Mama."

"How thoughtful of them," I said. I tried to hold back

my joy because I didn't want to make Boone feel bad.

He smiled. "Yes, it was. What's for supper?" He winked at me.

It was then I noticed a pot of something on the stove.

"Your mother is the best! It's beef stew. And bread!"

"Looks like we'll feast like kings tonight." He chuckled as I dished up the meal.

Then he prayed over it, thanking God for our family and for providing for us. Then we enjoyed the meal in our newly furnished home.

CHAPTER 26

January 5, 1891

BOONE

The morning I was scheduled to leave to survey the Rock Butte route for the railroad, Jaclyn woke early with me. She started making eggs but ran outside quickly. I hurried to the stove to keep the eggs from burning. When they looked normal, I dumped them onto a plate and started eating them.

"Sorry," she said as she came back inside. "The smell." She held her nose.

I felt her forehead. Her skin was clammy. "Should I delay my trip for a few days?"

She continued to hold her nose. "No, you need to go."

I frowned as she handed me the biscuits she baked yesterday.

"I don't feel up to cooking more for you. I'm sorry. My stomach is..."

She ran outside again.

I sighed and took one biscuit from the container. It tasted just like Mama's, all fluffy and delicious.

I cleaned the pan and plate that I used. Hopefully, any lingering smell dissipated.

Jaclyn entered the house again. I handed her a glass of water.

"Here. Are you sure you don't want me to stay?"

"Go. I'll be fine."

She shivered.

"You are not alright. Lay down." I grabbed the throw blanket off the back of the couch and laid it over her before I stoked the fire.

"I'll stop by Eddie's shop and ask Annabel to check on you. If you feel worse, send for Mama, you hear me."

She nodded.

After I grabbed my things, I headed over to the office. By the time I arrived, Holt already unlocked the office. Dustin, Charlie, and Silas waited inside. Once we packed the gear, we delivered it to the train station.

"Did Jack give you any trouble about staying behind?" Silas asked. I thought it was interesting how he switched between calling her Jack and Jaclyn all the time.

"No. She's sick."

Silas frowned.

"My cousin that owns the butcher shop is going to check on her and send for Mama if she gets worse."

The rest of the trip to Ash Fork, I worried about her. I hated to leave her alone in town, especially since she felt ill.

Once we arrived in Ash Fork, Silas's crew of ten was ready to go. We set out southwest of Ash Fork toward the Rock Butte area. The ground sloped slightly in elevation as we rode across the desert. Dirt, scrub brush, and dry grass covered the expanse as we moved ever closer to the butte.

At camp, one of Silas's assistants drew a map of the ground we covered that day while the cook gathered firewood and the wrangler cared for the horses and mules. It was nice having the extra help.

The next day we pressed further into the mountain terrain. Silas and I agreed to split into two parties and to meet back at the main camp in one week. I took Holt, Charlie, Dustin, and Giovanni, or as we called him, the Sicilian. The five of us scouted what we thought was the harder route. We went on horseback and carried only a minimum number of provisions.

We climbed steadily in elevation on the first day, and the wind turned colder and whipped through my coat. The terrain grew rugged and became difficult to traverse. Jagged rock formations jutted up on both sides of a deep ravine. The trail we blazed was nestled between a tall limestone rock face and a steep slope down to the ravine. When we found a clearing large enough to make camp, we did despite the early hour.

Since plenty of daylight remained, Holt and I explored for another hour. I sketched out a rough map as we went, which slowed us down. After an hour, we backtracked to our camp.

Relief washed over me when I saw they built a fire. I took care of Outlaw before I tied him with the other horses. Then I stood by the fire to warm up. The temperature continued to drop.

"Kinda wish we brought our tents," Dustin said. "It's gonna be a cold one."

"We have enough wood to keep the fire burning at night?" I asked.

"Sure thing, boss," Charlie said as he handed me a mug of beans and a spoon.

I ate one of Jaclyn's biscuits. Mmm. Still soft after a few days on the trail. Surely, Mama gave her the recipe. I wrapped my blanket around my shoulders as the temperature dropped.

"How's Jack?" Holt asked.

"She was sick when I left." I brushed some crumbs off my pants. I hoped Annabel helped her. A stab of guilt pierced my heart. I could have delayed the trip a few days.

Holt nodded. "Always hard to leave the family, but even harder when you know you're leaving them at a bad time."

I cleared my throat. "Other than that, she's doing well. I want to involve her with the business in town, so I ordered another transit that should arrive while we're gone. She can accept local work or start on the station site."

Charlie slapped me on the shoulder. "Good idea. I'm sure she'll like it."

I smiled. "I'm having it delivered to Jack Colter, so she'll get a laugh out of that."

The men chuckled, even the Sicilian.

"She's a feisty one," the Sicilian said. "When Silas told me she married you, I didn't believe it. She's too wild to be tied down."

I snorted. "Well, believe it. I'm shocked she didn't fight with me about staying home."

"Maybe she's a—what do you call it—stone away," the Sicilian said.

"Stowaway?" Dustin offered.

"That's it! Stowaway."

"Unless you know something I don't," I said, "not this time."

The Sicilian laughed. "I remember our first trip after her mama died. Silas did not bring her along. Instead, she was a stowaway. We had a wagon full of supplies, and she hid in there for two whole days before we found her."

He shook his head. "She's sneaky, that one."

I laughed. "Maybe I should have checked the mule packs before we left the main camp."

"That same trip was when she shot her first deer. Silas, me, and a few others taught her how to hunt. I was with her when she shot it. Perfect aim. I showed her how to field dress it. Didn't know if she'd like hunting or not. She surprised us when she enjoyed it and did not get sick."

My Jaclyn could do just about anything she set her mind to. She would be fine. I hoped.

The next morning, we left at first light. We hurried past the area that Holt and I scouted the night before. Once we made it to a new place, our pace slowed to allow me time to draw the map and for Holt to study the rocks.

Around noon, the trail narrowed considerably as clouds gathered overhead. We found a spot to tie the horses. Then we proceeded on foot. What looked like a trail earlier in the day eventually disappeared, so we started our own. On our left, the smooth rock face towered above us. On our right, the land sloped steeply to the ravine we skirted the entire trip.

The Sicilian led the way. As the trail narrowed, I considered turning back. My gut told me there was not enough of a ledge to continue safely.

All a sudden, Giovanni's foot slipped. He slid over the edge and down the steep embankment.

"Gio!" I hollered when he settled onto a narrow ledge far below.

"Boone!" he shouted back. His voice sounded strained.

"Dustin, get the rope from camp. Holt, do you see another way down? Charlie, ideas?"

My eyes scanned the surrounding area. No boulders or trees to anchor a rope. I took a few steps forward and peered around the rock formation in front of us. Nothing there either. I should have made him turn around.

"Hold on, Gio!" Charlie shouted.

"Let's backup," I said. "There's nothing in front of us that will help."

As we walked back the way we came, Holt found a safe place to scale down the side of the slick slope with the rope. I wasn't sure how to rescue Giovanni, but I needed to try. I couldn't leave him.

"Let's anchor it on this tree," Charlie suggested.

"Tie it around you, Boone," Holt said. "You got a wife at home that won't be none too pleased with us if we lose you."

I never feared for my life. Not once. But the thought of not returning to Jaclyn created additional stress within me. A part of me wished Holt said nothing.

I tightened my gloves, and double checked the rope.

"Here goes nothing," I said. I leaned back and repelled down the side of the slick rock face to the ledge barely wider than the length of my foot. Snow fell as the wind grew colder.

The Sicilian laid on the wider section of the ledge about twenty yards away. In order to get to him, I had to let go of the rope. I secured it with a rock. Then I slowly made my way to him.

"Gio!"

He turned and looked at me. He groaned but did not move.

Then I saw it and coughed. The bone from his leg stuck out of his skin with sharp jagged edges. Blood pooled around him. My stomach tightened.

As I neared, he shook his head. "Leave me."

"Not a chance."

"I can't walk. I can't climb." He pointed to his arm

which hung at an unnatural angle. "You go home to Jack. Leave me."

When I reached him, I rolled him over and saw that his back landed on a large rock. I pressed on his legs. Nothing. I pressed on his stomach. Nothing. His back was probably broken.

"I'm done for. Go home to Jack."

Snow stuck to his hat and melted into the pool of his blood. I stared into his dark eyes as the grim truth settled in my heart.

"Get my gun. Put it in my left hand."

My stomach lurched. He asked me to help him end his life. I didn't want to.

"Boone. You must do this."

"Giovanni." I shook my head.

"Please."

He tried to push himself up, but he was too weak or his broken back stopped him.

I cursed. Even if I got him up the cliff and back to our base camp and then back to Ash Fork, no doctor could fix a broken back or his shattered leg. I glanced away to delay the decision.

"Boone."

I kneeled next to him.

"I'm so sorry, Giovanni."

I took his pistol and loaded it.

"Say a prayer for me."

I coughed to clear my throat. Nothing came to mind, so I recited the twenty-third Psalm to him. He smiled when I said the part about fearing no evil in the shadow of the valley.

"For you are with me." I coughed to dislodge the sorrow from my throat. "Your rod and your staff, they comfort me."

I sniffed and somehow finished reciting the Psalm that Mama drilled into my head as a young boy.

"You're a good man. Jack is lucky to have you. Tell Luca I love him and am proud that he followed in my footsteps. It's been a pleasure working with him."

A tear slid from my eye. I wiped it away.

"Go, now. Leave me."

As snow covered his legs, I turned away and abandoned the Sicilian on that ledge. The image burned its way deep into my mind. When I arrived at the rope, I heard the shot echo against the canyon walls, and I flinched.

"Boone!" Holt called down to me. "You alright?"

"I'm coming back up!"

After I wrapped the rope around my waist, I started the climb, and willed my emotions to stay buried. The cold made the rock slicker than on the way down. My hand found no secure hold. My foot lost its grip. I fell.

The rope pulled taut, and the air squeezed from my lungs before I slammed hard against the rock face. My limbs went limp. Blackness swallowed me.

CHAPTER 27

JACLYN

After I recovered from the flu earlier in the month, I spent weekdays at the office. I busied myself by studying maps of the town, planning future trips, and thinking about how we could drum up more business in town.

I tried to wait patiently for Boone to return, but he was gone for three solid weeks. He was due back last Thursday. Somehow, I got through the weekend. By Monday, my worries turned to fear. I imagined all kinds of terrible things that could have happened to him.

As I paced the length of the office again, I sighed. No news did not mean something bad happened.

Lord, please protect him and all the men. Keep them safe and bring them home soon.

To keep myself busy, I dusted the cabinets, reorganized the papers on the desk, and double checked the math on our report, not once but three times. Then I drank my seventh cup of coffee.

The train whistle blew in the distance. I looked at the clock. Half-past two. I donned my coat, grabbed my reticule, and locked up the office.

My feet wanted to run to the train, but I told myself to walk normally. He probably wasn't even on it. It could be a waste of time.

When I arrived at the station, people disembarked the train. I scanned every face in the crowd. A tall broad-shouldered man exited. I couldn't see his face. Then a young woman ran to him. It wasn't Boone.

My heart dropped to the station platform. I took a deep breath to hold back my tears as I touched the compass pin at my neck. Boone, you promised you would return to me.

Then I sat on a bench and watched passengers pick up their horses. No black stallion. No Boone.

A verse from Philippians came to mind. "Do not be anxious," I whispered. "Present my requests to God. With thanksgiving."

I sighed. *Lord, I know he is in your hands. Thank you for watching over him. Please help me trust you.*

I sat there until every person left the platform before I returned to the office.

"Hey, Jaclyn!" Vi greeted me as I unlocked the door.

"Vi!" I hugged her close.

"Still no word?"

I shook my head.

"Mama is worried too. She asked me to stop by after school to see how you are doing."

"I'm trying to trust God. It's not as easy as it should be."

Vi laughed. "Mama would agree with you."

"Excuse me," a burly man said as he stepped down from a wagon. "I have a crate here for Jack Colter."

I raised an eyebrow and glanced at Vi. "That's me."

"Where do you want it?"

After I opened the door for the man, he and another man set the crate down in an empty spot before they left.

"Jack?" Vi asked.

"My papa calls me that sometimes."

"Well," she said as she gave me one last hug, "I better head on home. Let us know when you hear from him or if you need anything."

"Thanks, Vi."

After she left, I retrieved a crowbar from the back room, and I pried the top off the crate. When I moved the straw aside, I blinked.

"Another transit?"

I carefully lifted the beautiful, shiny brass piece of equipment from its straw nest. I set up the wooden tripod legs. Then I attached the single vernier transit to the top. It was the '74 Gurley, just like Boone's other one.

Was it for me?

After picking up the lid of the crate, I verified the shipping label. Jack Colter. That could only be for me.

When had Boone ordered it? Perhaps, he intended to let me survey. Warmth flooded my soul. My husband bought me a transit.

My fingers ran over the smooth polished site. My career wasn't over. A smile stretched across my lips as my excitement grew. I planned to accept local jobs. I could even survey the train station site.

Since I would need an assistant, I posted a "help wanted" sign in the window.

The clock read half-past three. I headed over to James's office for his new secret railroad. I discovered he left his old job last fall.

"Jaclyn, is something wrong?" he asked when he closed the door behind me.

"Boone isn't back yet."

He frowned.

"That's not why I'm here. I wanted to see if you have plans for," I lowered my voice, "a station location."

"Care for a walk?"

I agreed despite the chill in the air.

"It will go at the end of Pleasant Street." James led me to the site. "The depot building will be roughly here. The right-of-way allows us to cut through to the northeast at an angle."

He walked me along the proposed path.

"We'll have a turntable, engine house, passenger depot, freight depot, and several other structures."

As we walked, I took notes to mark the streets, and I drew small symbols to represent the various structures.

"I can start surveying for the depot, if you'd like."

James turned to look at me and raised one eyebrow.

"I have plenty of experience and I can be discreet."

"Alright. When you have the report ready, let me know."

I smiled as a plan formed in my mind.

———

Finally, on Friday, a young man entered the office.

"I saw your sign," he said. He looked into my eyes. "You have different colored eyes."

I was used to people commenting on my eyes. "Yes, I do. My name is Jaclyn Colter. And you are?"

"Loren Harrison."

I studied the young man. His lanky form looked sturdy enough for the job. His dark eyes scanned the room. He wore work trousers and a cotton shirt underneath a dark wool coat. He might be a little older than me, but his face held a youthful appearance.

"You ever work for a surveyor?" I asked.

"No. I mostly helped with my papa's freight business."

"Ah, right. J.W. Harrison & Co."

He nodded. "That's the one."

"Well, for the immediate future, I need an assistant to help as I survey sites around town. You'll carry the transit, help set it up, and manage a measuring tape."

He frowned. "Never done those things."

"That's alright. I'll teach you."

A hint of a smile graced his lips. "You said your last name is Colter?"

"Yes. I'm Boone's wife."

His dark eyes rounded wide. "Boone? Tall beefy guy?"

I laughed. "That's the one."

"Ha. Most of us in school didn't think he'd ever marry."

I glanced away. "Well, we are."

"He around? I'd love to say hi. It's been a few years."

"He's up north surveying a site for our client." Until I knew if I could trust Loren, I kept our client's identity a secret. "Are you available today? I've been itching to get started with the job."

He agreed, and he carried the transit and measuring tape over to the site. "You know, my papa has this mini-wagon called a handcart. I'll make one for you since we'll work on jobs around town. It'd make carting supplies easier."

I smiled. I liked he thought of ways to make the job simpler.

As I set up the transit, I showed him how to put it together. I took it apart and placed it back in the case. Then I had him try. He remembered the steps perfectly, even how to level the equipment properly.

After I demonstrated how to work with the steel tape and plumb bob, we took measurements of the area for the new train depot. We worked well together.

At the end of the day, I told Loren to come back on Monday so we could complete the train depot site survey. He carried all the equipment back to the office. I paid him and set up a schedule for his future paychecks. He also walked me home, since it was on his way back to his parents' place.

When I entered my house, I sighed. Still no Boone. He was more than a week overdue. I touched the gold pin from him again as I could not shake the feeling that something terrible happened.

CHAPTER 28

BOONE

When I woke up, I did not recognize where I was. I took a deep breath and pain seared my lungs. A firm hand on my shoulder kept me from sitting up.

"Easy now," Holt said. "You had a pretty hard fall."

As my muscles contracted over my ribs, I moaned in pain when he helped me sit up.

"Bet you got a few cracked ribs in there," Charlie said. "Especially given the way the rope caught your fall."

"Gio. He's gone," I said. Somehow, I was still alive.

Charlie nodded.

"We gotta get you back to the main camp. We're late re-turning," Holt said.

"How long was I out?"

"Two days," Dustin said.

I tried to stand but the pain in my chest and lungs stopped me.

"Dustin's got a travois ready. Don't think you'll make it up on your horse," Holt said.

Dustin laid it next to me and I rolled onto it. He hooked it up to his horse. Smart. Outlaw was a magnificent horse, but he hated anything hitched to him.

We made slow progress, and I faded in and out of consciousness. When I woke, the pain came in sharp waves with every breath. My arms were sore. I could feel bruises on my legs and back. One time I woke, I felt my face. Pretty sure cuts and bruises covered it.

After three more days, we finally arrived back at the base camp. Only the wrangler and cook were there.

"Where's Silas?" I asked as I tried to stand.

Holt stopped me, and he set up my tent around where I lay. Once the blanket was over me, I fell asleep again.

The next time I woke, Silas and his crew were in camp. He entered my tent to check on me.

"Sorry about Gio," I said. "He said…" I winced in pain as I tried to take a deep breath. "To let Luca know he loves him and is proud that he followed in his footsteps."

"I'll tell him. Just concentrate on feeling better."

"What day is it?"

Silas rubbed a hand over his beard. "January thirtieth."

My eyes went wide. I tried to sit up, but the pain flattened me. "I need to get back to Jaclyn."

Silas sighed. "You will. Just not until next week. We need a few more days to complete the route before we head back. That should save you another trip. Holt didn't think you had any life-threatening injuries. You should be fine."

"Alright. Use my crew if it helps speed things up."

Silas agreed.

After three more days, I could finally stand without help, though packing up the tent wore me out. By the time I sat atop Outlaw, I wanted to lie down again.

We arrived in Ash Fork on Friday, February sixth early in the morning, over two weeks after I told Jaclyn I would be home. She must be worried sick.

That day, Silas's crew returned to California, while he returned to Prescott with us. By the time the train pulled into the station, I was exhausted.

"Boss, we'll take care of everything. You head home. We'll make sure Outlaw makes it to the livery."

Since it was on my way home, I trudged toward the office. I looked up as I walked past the window. Jaclyn sat at the desk pointing to something on a map. A thin man stood close beside her, bent over her shoulder looking at the map. My jaw twitched as I opened the door.

The man straightened and smiled at me. I wondered if he knew it was my wife he leaned over much closer than I liked.

She looked up.

"Boone!"

Then she bolted to her feet, ran to me, and practically tackled me in a hug. I moaned at the pain that seared through my lungs, but I held her tight as I glared at the stranger.

"I was so worried. I thought something bad must have happened."

I stroked her hair as I closed my eyes. "Something bad happened."

She released me. Her eyes traveled my length. "You're hurt. Sit down."

I took the closest chair.

"What happened?"

The thin man with dark eyes stepped forward. "Boone." He held out his hand. Then I recognized him from my school days.

"Loren," I said flatly.

"Good to see you. Sorry you were injured."

I glanced at Jaclyn.

"Loren applied for our open position to assist me with surveying around town."

I narrowed my eyes and crossed my arms. Even though they respected Loren in the community, he spent so much time alone with my wife while I was gone that I didn't like it.

"Loren," Jaclyn said, "I think we'll pick this up on Monday. Thank you for your help."

Loren nodded and left as the crew arrived.

"Boss, you need to go home," Holt said.

Jaclyn tugged on my arm. "Come on. Holt can lock up. Let's get you home and cleaned up."

I didn't resist. "Your father came back, too."

"He did? Oh, good. I will see if he wants to join us for supper after church on Sunday."

As soon as we were home, she asked, "What happened, Boone?"

"We lost the Sicilian."

She set a mug of coffee in front of me as I looked away. I could still see Giovanni's broken and battered body. As I remembered the sound of the gunshot that took his life, I flinched. I propped my elbows on the table and rested my head in my hands. When I coughed, pain shot through my ribs.

Jaclyn stood next to me and rubbed my back. I heard her sniff and knew without looking that she cried over the loss.

"He was a good man," she whispered.

"I'm sorry, Jaclyn. I should have told him to turn back."

"It's not your fault. It's a dangerous job. He knew that. We all know that."

As I wrapped my arms around her waist, I buried my face against her stomach. Then uncharacteristically I shed a few tears. She ran her fingers through my hair and murmured soothing sounds to me.

At length, she pulled away and sat next to me. "Thank you for coming back."

My lips pressed together in a thin line. "I'm sorry."

"Should I call the doctor? Have you seen one yet?"

I shook my head.

"Go lie down in bed."

"But I'm filthy."

She laughed. "Well, I can wash the sheets tomorrow. You go rest."

I nodded as I shuffled toward the bedroom. I kicked off my boots and laid down on top of the blanket.

Sometime later, the doctor arrived. He said my ribs were cracked. Lots of bruising. Nothing else was busted. He left some willow bark powder for me.

Jaclyn warmed water for a bath, so I undressed with her help. As she scrubbed my back for me, she let out a little gasp.

"What exactly happened to you? You're covered with bruises."

"I climbed down to Gio. When I tried to climb back up, I slipped. Or as I like to call it, I pulled a Jack."

She snorted. "So, you hit the side of a cliff and knocked yourself out."

I gave her a wry smile. "Something like that."

Before she said anything else, I dunked my head under the water to wash out my hair and beard. When I came up for air, she towel-dried my hair.

"I'm just glad you made it home safely."

I stood and let the water drip from my body. Then I toweled off.

"When did you hire Loren?" I tried to keep the edge from my voice as I threw on an undershirt and trousers.

"Are you angry? You bought me a transit, so I put it to use, and I needed the help."

I sighed and swallowed my jealousy. "It's fine. What did you survey?"

"The site for the new train station."

"So, you've talked to James."

"Yes. Loren and I are almost done with the report for the train depot."

I smiled and pulled her close. "I guess it was an excellent investment after all."

She smiled up at me. "Yes, it was. I'm taking on other work in town."

Then I captured her sweet lips with mine and kissed her softly for several minutes. As longing rose, I ended the kiss and rested my forehead against hers.

"You scared me, Boone." She blinked rapidly but a few tears escaped and trailed lines down her face. I wiped them away.

"I scared me." The admission rolled off my tongue.

After a minute, she cleared her throat. "Why don't you rest while I make some supper and mix up some willow bark powder for you."

I released my hold on her and laid down in bed.

When supper was ready, she woke me, and I joined her at the table. I was famished, and the roast tasted amazing.

"This is delicious."

She snorted. "Of course it tastes good. You've been on the trail for a month."

"No, it'd taste just as delicious if I had been home."

"I hope you don't mind," she said, "but I've kinda taken over your office. I organized your paperwork, paid the bills out of the money I had, and started advertising for more work in town."

"I'll add you to the account tomorrow. Before I left, I should have done that." The guilt hung on my shoulders. Some husband I turned out to be. I continued to fail her.

"I managed fine. Your family was great. Vi, Annabel, and your mama checked on me often. I should send word that you're back. Your mama has been quite worried too."

After supper, I helped her with dishes, despite her protests. Then I retired to bed early, grateful to be home and alive and that my wife was healthy and safe.

CHAPTER 29

JACLYN

On Monday morning, the office buzzed with activity. Holt, Charlie, Dustin, Boone, and my papa all came in. Papa cleaned his transit. Holt and Charlie tried to find a place to write up reports. Dustin cleaned Boone's transit. Boone sulked and frowned a lot. Especially at Loren.

"Boone," I said, "why don't you find us a few more desks. We can afford it since James paid us for the completed reports."

He sighed and scuffed out of the office with a glance over his shoulder. I held back a sigh. I thought he was fine with me working, but he the way he glared at Loren left me wondering if he really was.

An hour later, he returned with a wagon full of three desks. Holt and Dustin unloaded them. I was glad Boone let them. He needed to take it easy with those busted ribs.

"Loren, you work on writing this up, like I showed you last week. Then we can review it."

"Yes, ma'am."

He sat down on the other side of the desk.

Boone came up next to me and placed his arm around

me possessively. At least that's how it seemed to me.

"What are you working on?" he asked.

"Loren's writing up the report for the depot. We were just reviewing some details on the map."

He studied the map. "How long have you worked on this?"

"Two weeks."

"That's it?"

I smiled up at him. "Come on, you already know I'm amazingly talented." I hoped for one of his deep bellied laughs. Instead, I received a thin smile.

"Would you like your desk back?" I asked as I stood.

"Looks to me like it's yours."

The edge in his voice hurt, and I'd had enough of his grousing.

"Take a walk with me," I said as I grasped his hand and led him out the front door.

"What's gotten into you? Do you not like Loren? Are you mad at me for doing exactly what I thought you wanted me to do?"

He sighed heavily and ran a hand through his hair.

"I don't know what I expected. On one hand, I'm thrilled that you've taken care of so much. On the other..."

I turned to face him. "What is it?"

"I guess I'm a little jealous of how much time Loren has spent with you."

Measuring my words, I said, "He is a quick learner. He seems to pick up on the smallest details. You and I both know what a valuable trait it is."

As I reached for his hands, I continued, "You, Boone, have nothing to fear from Loren. You are the only man who has space in my heart besides my papa. Loren is an excellent employee. With the right mentoring, either from

one of us or Papa, he could become a great assistant survey-
or."

He nodded. "You're right. I need to adjust my attitude."

Then he laced his fingers with mine as we walked to the
train depot site. "Tell me about it."

I explained James's plans and where the various buildings
would go. By the time I was done, Boone caught my excitement.

"Thank you," I said.

"For what?"

"The transit. Letting me be a part of your business. I'm
sorry if I took over. I just saw things that needed done and I
did them."

He laughed, and my heart warmed. "I am not upset
about that. Your presence in the office will make our business a success. I didn't know I needed your help, but you've
proven I do."

Taking a deep breath, I ventured the question I wanted
to avoid. "When will you go out again?"

"Not for three or four weeks. I need to be in top shape.
Silas kept us out longer so he could finish the work for the
alternate route through Rock Butte. Our next leg will be
from Rock Butte down through Granite Dells. I need to
meet with James to understand where he has the right-of-
way."

"Will it go through Colter Ranch?" I asked.

He looked away. "I have a feeling it will. The tension
will add to my family dynamics, and I don't look forward to
it. I won't take sides. Unfortunately, Papa and Sam will see
it that way because I agreed to survey it."

He turned to me. "With a family to provide for, I won't
turn away work."

"I'm sorry. Can you talk to James?"

"I will. Judging by the trajectory of the line from the depot, it will probably cross through a corner of the ranch."

When we returned to the office, all the men quietly wrote up reports on their various specialties. It was almost lunchtime.

"Jack," Papa said. "Can I take you out to lunch?"

"Of course. Should we bring back food for everyone?"

Boone shook his head. Holt held up a pail. Charlie pointed to his. Dustin and Loren shook their heads. I guess everyone brought their lunch.

"Boone, you can eat my sandwich," I teased him as I left with Papa.

Papa took me to a little café nearby. Once we ordered, he opened the conversation.

"I sent my resignation to the State of California."

"Oh, no! You love your job."

He smiled and squeezed my hand. "Not as much as I love my daughter. I want to live near you, Boone, and my future grandchildren."

My cheeks warmed as I realized, his grandchildren might be closer at hand than I considered.

"Besides, Boone has more work than he can handle. If he hires more men, I can help train them. We'll shape up his crew for expeditions. You and Loren, or maybe Dustin, can keep things moving in town."

I laughed. "Papa, are you taking over my husband's business?"

He shook his head. "No, but I am offering to help my son-in-law strengthen his business, just like you already have, by bringing my skills and talents and offering them to him. I think I can help mentor him too, without being an overbearing father-in-law."

I smiled. "So, you're really staying?"

He nodded.

"I'm so glad. I really missed you."

The rest of the week passed quickly. James invited us to supper at the end of the week.

When we entered his home, I tried not to gape. It was massive, at least three to four times the size of our home. Dark wood floors greeted us. An expensive crystal light fixture lit the entryway which was a room as large as our living room. Gold and brass accents dotted expensive looking end tables and the mantle in his parlor. Boone handed James the reports, and he set them on a side table, before James showed us back to the dining room.

"That's the depot report and the alternate route from Ash Fork to Rock Butte," Boone said.

"Good. We'll settle up after supper."

The china plates were edged in gold. Ornate silverware sat next to the plates. A similar crystal and gold chandelier lit the room, casting a shine on the polished dark wood table. Eight chairs lined the length of the table.

A Mexican woman appeared and set out several dishes on the table.

"Thank you, Maria," he said as he held out a chair for me. I sat, feeling very underdressed in my work dress. I wished I had worn my purple silk Sunday dress.

"You look lovely, Jaclyn. You have a glow about you," James said.

"Thank you." Heat warmed my cheeks.

"Guess being married to my wild brother agrees with you."

Boone laughed. "Being married to her agrees with me."

James said a prayer over the meal. That surprised me because he rarely appeared at church and how Boone described him made me think James was not very devout.

When he finished, he offered me some roast chicken.

"I like what you've done with the office," he said. "Seems like you have it organized and ready to grow."

I thanked him and passed the plate across the table to Boone. Once we were served, I started eating.

"Tell me the plan for the line between Rock Butte and here." Boone said.

"I'd like to run it as straight south as we can. Frank wants to link up a feeder line to Jerome so we can pick up the ore from the mines there. It's not clear yet if we would build the feeder or the mine would."

Boone nodded. "What about Granite Dells into Prescott?"

James sighed. "Try as I might, I don't think we'll be able to avoid the ranch completely. Find the best route, but if it goes through part of the ranch, so be it. The territorial government will side with us."

I frowned. James sounded so calloused. It was his family's land.

He glanced at me. "Don't mistake my tone for a lack of empathy. If I could keep it from going through Colter land, I would. It's not possible. I'm hoping you can find an easy, cost-effective way to minimize the impact to Colter land. I'm not looking forward to a war with Papa or Sam."

"Me either," Boone said.

"I know. I'm hoping they will forgive us in time."

The rest of supper, Boone told stories about his latest trip. He left out the most frightening parts of his fall and injury. James seemed engaged.

Finally, James shook his head. "You always cheat death. I hope the good Lord continues to keep it that way."

"Me, too," I said under my breath as James escorted us to the parlor so he could review our reports. He asked several questions before he paid us for our work. Then he said his farewells.

"Happy Valentine's Day," Boone said as he walked me home. "Sorry I didn't realize it until right now."

"It is? I guess I forgot too."

He opened the door to the house. "I can think of a few ways to celebrate if you're interested."

He closed the door and pulled me into his arms.

"What did you have in mind?" I teased as I knew very well what he meant. It was a fine Valentine's evening.

CHAPTER 30

BOONE

The middle of March came quicker than I expected. My business fell into a rhythm. Silas and I planned the expedition from Rock Butte down to Granite Dells. We hired several more men for the crew and spent much of the month training them. Holt mentored a young man named Aiken Dudley in geology and mineralogy. Loren brought his younger brother, Allan with him. Allan understood plant life well, so Charlie worked with him.

Pearl Harrison, Loren's sister, hung around and Jaclyn taught her, while Silas took Dustin under his wing, and I started working with Loren. It pleased me that my wife partnered with an eighteen-year-old woman instead of a twenty-two-year-old unmarried man.

On March sixteenth, I packed my things for our next trip. As Jaclyn set breakfast in front of me, she laid a hand on my shoulder. I looked up, concerned.

"I have some news for you," she said. "We're going to have a child."

I blinked. I coughed. The words failed to make sense to me.

COLTER SONS BOOK 2

She frowned. "I thought you might be happy."

When she turned and rounded the table, I reached for her arm.

"A baby?"

She nodded.

While I hugged her to mask my alarm, I swallowed hard and forced a smile I did not feel. A child. That was a whole passel of responsibility that I felt unprepared to handle.

When she pulled away and sat down, I smiled with a little more sincerity. I searched for the right words. "How far along are you?"

"Almost four months."

Ash Fork. Sometime around December. I swallowed the eggs that turned to tasteless mush in my mouth.

She looked down at her plate and pushed her food around.

"I'm sorry." Those words often came from my lips as a married man. I never apologized as much as I did since marrying.

"It just took me by surprise is all. It's wonderful news." I tried to add some enthusiasm to my tone, but it came out sounding strained.

"We'll need to clean up the other room if it is to become a nursery."

I nodded. "We have some time, right? I can clean it out when I get back."

"Do you mind if I share the news with your family?"

I smiled. "Please do. I'm sure it will excite Mama. And we already know your father will be tickled."

She laughed. "Yes, he will. Please tell him when you see him this morning."

I nodded my agreement and took my empty plate to the sink. Then I pulled her into my arms and kissed her soundly. "Be safe while I'm gone. Don't push yourself too hard."

"I won't. Besides, I'll have Pearl's help."

Then I picked up my things and headed to the livery to retrieve Outlaw and rent a few mules.

It made no sense to take the train that time. Rock Butte was too far from any of the Central Arizona Railway stops. Instead, we traveled by road and trails until we met up with where Silas and his crew left off in February.

We made quick work over the land between Rock Butte and Granite Dells. For once, our trip was uneventful. Our new crew members were eager to learn.

When we arrived near Granite Dells and set foot on Colter land, I was not as ready as I hoped for a confrontation. Sam, Deacon, Papa, Warren Cahill, and several of the cowboys came into our camp the morning after we arrived.

"Morning," I said as I studied each of them. Sam wore his gun belt. Sam never wore his gun belt.

I frowned. "Expecting trouble?" I asked as I nodded toward him.

"Depends. Are you going to get off our land?" Sam asked.

I stepped forward and pulled Sam aside.

"Look, we're here on a job. These men, I, we all have families we are supporting with this job. We don't decide where the line goes."

"You don't? Sure seems like it from here."

"Sam, I'm not trying to cause trouble for you. You're my brother. Papa is my father. I'm trying to minimize the impact to your land."

"Go around it." Sam crossed his arms over his chest.

"I can't. I will keep it as far north and west as I can, but the geography of the area will determine the route."

Sam narrowed his eyes. He shoved me. "I can't believe

you dare to call yourself a Colter!"

I blinked. I could not recall a time where Sam raised his voice to anyone, much less initiated physical contact. If he wasn't my brother, I would have knocked him flat on the ground.

"Step back, Sam. Go home to your wife and sons."

Deacon stepped forward and grabbed Sam's arm. "Let's not fight. Boone's just doing his job."

For once I appreciated Deacon's meddling.

Sam spit at my feet as Deacon dragged him away from the camp. Papa frowned but mounted his horse. Warren and Sam followed him. Then Deacon was the last to leave.

"They wouldn't actually shoot at us, would they?" Holt asked.

I shook my head.

"I hope not," Silas said. "They seemed like good people when I stayed with them last fall."

The look on Papa's face hurt the most. He was more than disappointed. He was disgusted. It wasn't my fault. Like I told Sam, I was there for a job to support my wife and future child. If they had issues with the route, they could take it up with Frank Murphy and James.

"Let's get started. The sooner we start, the sooner we'll be on our way."

Three days later, as we packed up camp, and moved off Colter land, Sam rode out by himself.

"Boone!"

He dismounted his horse and struggled to catch his breath.

"Go."

"Sam, we're packing up now, alright!"

He shook his head. "It's Jaclyn."

My heart slammed into my chest.

"What?"

"She's… You have to go. She's at the doctor's."

My wife. The baby.

My feet flew to Outlaw. In one swift motion, I mounted my horse. I pressed him for speed along the back way to town. My throat constricted as I neared.

Lord, please don't take her from me.

CHAPTER 31

JACLYN

On the morning of April tenth, I woke feeling under the weather. My back felt sore most of the night and I tossed and turned. My neck hurt. I chalked it up to being almost five months pregnant.

I rubbed my extended belly. "Go easy on your mama today, you hear?"

A sharp pain left me breathless for a moment. It was as if he resisted my request. I smiled. I just assumed my little rascal was a he. He would be the spitting image of his wild father, I imagined, because of the difficulties he put me through.

I put on my shoes and tied them. Then I stood and made a piece of toast.

My stomach flipped and flopped while I walked toward the office.

"You look pale. Are you sure you're up to working today?" Pearl asked.

"I'll be fine."

She raised an eyebrow but did not debate further. I rubbed my back as we hiked up the hill southeast of the downtown. The town asked us to map lots for homes. Large juniper and pine trees covered the site, so we spent most of the day in the shade which I appreciated since I felt warm, and my back continued to ache.

When we sat down for lunch, I splashed some water on my face and neck.

"Maybe we should come back on Monday. You don't look so good."

"I'll be fine," I said as I set my uneaten sandwich aside. I stood and picked up the transit.

"Let me move it. You rest for a while longer."

I thanked Pearl. She was such a sweet young lady.

When she placed the transit in the new location, I found my landmark and lined up the site before I read the markings on the transit.

A wave of dizziness washed over me. A sharp pain tore through my abdomen. I buckled and crashed into the transit. It fell to the ground as I landed on it.

"Jaclyn!" Pearl yelled.

I looked up at her.

"You're bleeding!"

My gaze traveled to where my hand rested. I moved my hand away. Blood soaked through my dress as I rolled off the transit.

"Don't get up. Stay here. Let me get some help."

Pearl grabbed the handcart and climbed in it. Then she used a stick to push it forward. She let it roll down the hill at a frightening speed. I would have laughed at the sight of her if pain didn't slice through my abdomen. It rolled to a stop in the distance.

"Hurry," I whimpered.

Her oldest brothers met her on the street. They must have seen her crazy stunt from their freight office.

Nausea overwhelmed me. I threw up.

The world spun out of control. I closed my eyes as another sharp pain forced a scream from my lips.

"Here you take her shoulders. I'll grab her feet." A male voice said.

"Boone?"

"No ma'am. It's me, Martin Harrison. Henry's here too. We've got you."

I screamed as I felt like my insides tore apart.

"Hang on, Jaclyn," Pearl said. "We're almost there."

"Boone." His name left my lips on a hoarse whisper.

Pain overwhelmed me. I felt myself lowered onto a table. I tried to open my eyes, but the pain stopped me. It lit a fire through my abdomen.

Tears streamed down my face when I finally understood that I lost my son.

"Mrs. Colter. Breathe this. It will help you relax."

Something was on my face. I breathed in and my body slackened. My eyes shut.

———

"Where is she!"

Boone.

My head ached. My eyes fluttered open as someone strok-ed my hair.

Boone's face came into view. He let out a long breath. "Thank God."

Tears trickled from his eyes before his beard swallowed them whole.

"What…"

The pain in my midsection. I felt like someone tackled me and beat my stomach over and over.

"The baby…"

I knew before Boone finished his thought. I was the worst mother because I lost my son.

The sadness in his eyes overwhelmed me, and I helplessly wept. My weeping turned into ugly, gut-wrenching sobs. Boone held me up and scooted onto the bed to rest my head against his chest. He rubbed his hand on my back.

When my sobs turned into wails, he held me with every ounce of strength and tenderness that he possessed. Wails ripped from my throat. I had no power to stop. My child was gone.

The doctor came back and gave me something before I slipped into unconsciousness again.

When I next woke, I was at home in our bed. The moment I made a slight movement, Boone stood over me.

"Jaclyn. Are you alright?"

Deep lines etched his forehead.

"No. I will never be alright!"

I looked away. I lost my child. It was my fault. I should have stayed home when I felt poorly. Instead, my stupid ambition took my son's life.

"Jaclyn, look at me."

I refused.

"Please." His voice was a whisper.

"You should have left me when you had the chance."

The bed shifted as he sat next to me. "Don't say that. I love you."

I pushed myself up. "How can you say that! I killed your son!" I pounded my fists against his chest. "Go away!"

His eyes widened in shock. He tried to hold me, but I shoved him away.

"Leave. Me. Alone."

"Boone," his mother's voice came from the doorway.

He glanced away from me but not before I saw the redness in his eyes. He stood and left the room.

Hannah entered and sat beside me. She held a damp cloth and dabbed it on my forehead.

"Jaclyn, don't blame yourself."

I snorted. "What do you know! You have six healthy grown children. Leave me alone."

She continued to dab my forehead and face. She cleared her throat. "I won't let you blame yourself for this."

Her words confused me. "You won't let me?! You don't know what it's like!"

Hannah took a deep breath. Her voice sounded far away when she spoke. "I lost my first child."

The fight left me as I turned to look at her.

"So, dear child, I know far more than you understand in this painful moment. I know the guilt that comes later. I know the blame. The regret. The incessant reliving of every action, every choice I made during that pregnancy. I tried to find the reason I lost my child."

I swallowed the lump in my throat. "I should have stayed home."

Hannah shook her head. "That would not have changed the inevitable. It only would have changed the location of where you lost him."

"It was a boy?"

She nodded. "The doctor thinks so. He wasn't sure."

The tears welled inside of me and spilled over. Sobs shook my body. My wails tore through the silence. Hannah laid a hand on my head. Then she whispered scripture and prayer over me.

I fell asleep again.

The next time I woke, Hannah helped me sit up.

"You need to eat something."

She held a spoonful of chicken noodle soup for me. I swallowed it. When she handed me the bowl, I ate slowly. Once I finished, she carried it to the kitchen before returning to my room.

"God is punishing me," I said.

She frowned.

"When I left California, my father wanted me to get married and have children. I didn't want that. I wanted to be a surveyor. So, God is finally punishing me for my rebellion."

Hannah sighed heavily. "That is not how He works. You know this. Those words are just your grief."

I looked away.

"I'm glad you are family. You are the only woman perfectly suited for my Boone."

I turned my head to meet her gaze.

"You have a fire in your soul, and you are good at your job. You've helped him build his business in a way that only you can."

She smiled. Then laughed. "Absolutely no one else could have tamed the worst parts of his wildness from him, like you have. And I have a feeling you didn't even try."

"He must hate me." Tears threatened to fall again. "I lost his son."

Hannah pressed her lips together and pushed my hair back from my face, like only a mother did. "He loves you more than life itself. He needs to see you soon. The only way you will both get through this loss is together."

She stood and kissed my forehead. "Get some rest."

I let the exhaustion pull me into a peaceful sleep.

In the middle of the night, I woke with a start. My chest tightened as I remembered what happened.

"Jaclyn?" Boone's groggy voice came from beside me.

"What is it?"

He lit the lamp next to the bed. Then he sat up and faced me.

Hannah was right. My husband's face showed his deep love and concern.

"I'm so sorry. I'm sorry I lost the baby. I'm sorry I yelled at you. I'm sorry I pushed you away."

His eyes softened. Then he turned down the lamp and pulled me down into the bed next to him. He laid his arm across me.

"Sleep, my love. There's nothing to forgive."

A lone tear rolled down my cheek as I snuggled closer to him. Just his presence comforted me.

CHAPTER 32

BOONE

A week after... I could not think the words. Despite not being ready to be a father, I carried my share of guilt over the loss of my son. I loved him even though I never met him. Perhaps not as much as Jaclyn did since she carried him for five months. She bonded with him. I loved him all the same.

So, a week later, I headed to the office. Silas and the crew arrived that afternoon. I sent word to Silas, but he worked through the grief of losing his first grandchild. I would have understood if he left the job unfinished, but he refused to.

When he dropped his things in the office, I suggested he head to my home to see Jaclyn.

"It will do her good to see you," I said. He promised to go see her as soon as he cleaned up.

I went through the motions of unpacking and cleaning my transit. Loren cleaned Silas's. The men seemed somber. They all knew what happened.

"How's Jaclyn?" Holt finally asked.

"She's getting better."

He nodded.

"Dustin," I said. "Would you be able to help me finish the job with the town tomorrow?"

"Sure thing, boss."

Dustin and I finished the survey in two days.

Silas already finished the report for the Rock Butte to Prescott section. I took it over to James's new office.

"I'm sorry for your loss," he said as he held the door open for me. "Mama stopped by to let me know a few days ago."

I nodded and took a seat across from his desk.

"How's Jaclyn?"

I sighed. Everyone wanted to know how she was doing. Didn't they realize my heart was broken too?

"She's fine."

James leaned forward. "And you?"

I coughed to hide the emotion. "Not good."

"I'm sorry. Mama thought you might not be taking it very well."

I never confided in my brother, but my words flowed.

"I'm devastated. I didn't think I was ready to be a father. But now that he's gone, a part of my heart has been ripped from me."

James gave me a sympathetic smile.

"I looked forward to arranging the nursery. The more I thought about him the more excited I got. Then…"

James nodded. "Then your wife's life was in danger, and you lost your son."

"Exactly!" I stood and paced the length of the room. I wanted to run. To ride Outlaw to the farthest reaches of the country. The pain was too much.

Instead, I fell onto the chair and held my head in my hands. James came and stood next to me. He squeezed my shoulder.

"It seems so unfair." My voice caught.

James let out a sardonic laugh as he sat in his chair again. "Life has never been fair. You know this."

I frowned at him.

"Come on, Boone. How is it that my two younger brothers get married before me?"

"We all thought you didn't want to get married," I confessed.

"My job keeps me too busy for a wife and family." He looked out the window. "But I wouldn't mind falling in love. You and Sam make it seem so easy."

I snorted. "Me? Do I need to remind you how I ended up married?"

"No. But you and Jaclyn love each other. When I see you in church—"

"I thought you didn't go."

"Well, I do. I just arrive after the first song and leave before the rest of you see me."

I wondered why James hid so much of himself. He perplexed me. It made no sense that he was jealous of me. Me. I married for all the wrong reasons.

"Anyway, when I see you and your wife together, I'll admit to feeling some envy. She looks at you like Ellie Mae looks at Sam. You are a different man with her. A better man."

I rubbed a hand over my beard as the truth of his words sank into my heart.

"So, yes, I'm sorry that you lost your son. I was kinda looking forward to being the uncle in town."

He flashed me one of his charming grins.

I snorted. "I'm not sure I would trust you alone with my child."

"Fair enough. I will enjoy it when you do finally have

children. You give me hope I might one day find someone to share my life."

"Speaking of family…" I told him about the encounter with Sam.

"I thought I caught a few icy stares from him when he was in town earlier this week."

"He's pretty upset."

"I hope when he sees what the railroad does for the town that he'll forgive me."

I sighed. "You haven't started construction yet. I'm not sure I can wait a few years for him to get over it."

"Just blame it on me."

I snorted.

"Oh, you already did. Well, tell me about the options to limit our footprint on Colter land."

I went over the report with him and told him I thought we could keep the railroad from going more than a few hundred yards into Sam's land. "It's not an area they use for grazing. If you're able to follow that route, then Sam should have no issues."

"Nice work."

After I finished walking him through the report, he paid me and then he invited me and Jaclyn to the celebration for the start of the Santa Fe, Prescott, & Phoenix Railway which was planned for the end of May.

"I'm not sure we'll come. I don't think Jaclyn will feel up to it."

"You're welcome to come. Even if it is at the last minute."

I thanked him and returned home to my wife.

When I opened the door, Jaclyn stood over the stove. She flashed me a weak smile. I took it.

"Glad to see you up and about," I said as I placed a kiss

on her cheek.

"Thank you for putting his things..." her voice broke.

I nodded. Then I hugged her. We stood there, content to draw strength from each other for several minutes before she stepped away to finish supper.

"Papa is coming for supper. I hope that's alright."

I smiled. "That will be nice."

Since I felt awkward, I chopped wood outside. We had plenty, but it felt good to do something useful.

By the time I returned inside, Silas arrived, and we sat down to eat. I prayed over the meal.

We talked about work and the plan for the next surveying trip.

"I think we should start on the route to Iron Springs as soon as possible," he said.

I agreed. To distract myself from my grief, I needed to work. I hoped it would help me move on. Perhaps my absence for a few weeks would help my wife too.

After Silas left, Jaclyn and I sat on the couch and stared into the fire. I placed my arm around her as she rested her head against me.

We survived some pretty crazy things in the six months we'd known each other. She nearly died in Hell Canyon. We married. I fought for her. She stayed with me. I nearly died at Rock Butte. We made it through those other times. I prayed we would make it through the loss of our son.

———

Church on Sunday was uncomfortable. Several friends asked about our loss. Vi talked to Jaclyn at length. Mama asked me how we were. Papa spoke to me for a few minutes. Sam glared at me and hurried his family home after service. Deacon and Grady gave their condolences and headed home.

Before I realized it, Jaclyn invited my parents and Vi home for supper. They walked with us to our house.

"Papa, I just want you to know that my recommendation to James was to cut across the northwest corner, not over two hundred yards into your land."

"Thank you. I will let Sam know."

"I don't want there to be bad blood between us."

Papa snorted. "You're my son. So, you and I will be fine."

"And Sam?"

"He's very protective of the ranch. Having sons will do that to a man. He sees a future for Sterling and Brody. He wants nothing to jeopardize that."

"I was just doing my job."

"I know that. Deep down he does too."

I sighed as Jaclyn set the food on the table. After I prayed, the conversation flowed around the table.

"Vi, how's school?"

She chatted about her friends and how she was looking forward to the summer. "Zayne Harrison is unbearable. I can't wait until school is out."

I smiled. I was pretty sure Zayne was sweet on Vi. Well, as sweet as a twelve-year-old could be. She might be sweet on him; with the way she went on about him. Mama smiled at me. I suspected she thought the same.

"When do you leave again?" Mama asked.

"Next week. Silas, me, and the crew are going to start the surveying for the route to Iron Springs. It should be a shorter trip. Just three weeks, I think."

Jaclyn glanced away. I worried how she would do while I was gone.

"Mama, can I stay with Jaclyn for a few weeks?"

Mama did not look the least bit surprised, which made me wonder if they discussed it earlier. "That's fine with me if Jaclyn wants the company."

"I suppose so," Jaclyn said softly. "I don't have another bed."

"I can sleep on the couch. I don't mind," Vi said.

"It's settled then," Papa said. "We'll drop her off after church next week."

"Alright," Jaclyn said.

When Mama hugged me goodbye, I thanked her.

"Don't thank me," she said. "It was all Vi's idea. She doesn't want her sister to be sad."

My heart warmed at my sister's kindness. I thanked her as I hugged her. She winked at me and said nothing more.

Leaving Jaclyn would be easier, knowing my family would care for her.

CHAPTER 33

JACLYN

"That Zayne Harrison!" Vi dramatically sighed and flopped onto a chair at my table.

I smiled. I was glad Vi stayed with me while Boone was gone. She kept me from wallowing too long in my sorrow over the loss of my baby.

"What did he do now?"

"He put a frog in my lunch pail. When I went to take my sandwich out, it licked my hand, and I dropped my lunch in the dirt. Everyone stared at me. When it jumped out, I shrieked."

I turned my back to make some tea for us so she wouldn't catch my smile. It was so cute how they pretended to hate each other. I wiped away my smile as I set a teacup in front of her.

"It was so embarrassing."

"I'm sorry." I coughed to hide my laughter. Then I quickly sipped my tea.

"Jaclyn, can I ask you a question?"

"Sure."

"Why does Preston drink so much?"

I took a deep breath and tried to gather my thoughts. No one knew why Preston drank. I tried to recall any conversations with my parents on the topic and came up empty. *Lord, give me words to explain it.*

"Some people have a deep sorrow," I started. "It haunts them, and they try to escape it. The drink numbs it for a while. When it wears off, they need more and more to numb the pain."

Vi swirled her tea.

"I imagine some even feel ashamed for turning to the drink and it drives them back to it."

"You are full of sorrow, but you don't drink."

My eyes burned. "Yes, I am grieving. And I'm trying to turn to God and friends, like you, for comfort instead of drowning my sorrow."

I dabbed at my eyes.

"How can I help Preston?"

I sighed heavily. "Besides prayer, I don't think we can do anything else. He has to want to change. Until he wants that, he won't change."

Vi came over and hugged me. "I'm sorry your baby died."

I sniffed. Then I let the tears fall as my sister comforted me.

After several minutes, I shook off my sorrow. "Let's get some supper started."

―――――

That night as I lay in bed, I pondered that conversation. Perhaps Boone ran from his sorrow by going out to the field so soon. I prayed for him, and that God would heal his grief too. As I prayed for our marriage, I prayed we would grow stronger through our loss. Then I prayed for my father. He wanted grandchildren so badly and our loss hurt him too.

Then I prayed for each of my in-laws. For Vi to grow into the woman God wanted her to be. That she would seek Him first and not let Zayne Harrison bother her so much.

Preston was a longer prayer. I asked God to help him want to change and deal with his sorrow or whatever drove him to drink his problems away. I prayed God would prepare him for what it would take to wake him up. Deep down, I knew it was a prayer that may take years or decades to answer, but I promised to pray for him whenever he came to mind.

Then I prayed for Hannah and Will. The next two were Deacon and Grady, followed by Sam and his family.

When my prayers turned to James, I wondered why he never married. The few times he invited Boone and me to his home, he seemed incredibly lonely. The bad blood between him and Sam bothered him. So, I prayed for that. And I prayed God would bring him a godly woman who would soften his heart and be as perfect for him as Boone was for me.

Then I prayed for my child that did not survive. I prayed for peace and healing of my heart. I prayed God would grant me the opportunity to be a mother and that I would be a good one.

CHAPTER 34

June 3, 1891

BOONE

I ran my hand through my hair, eager to arrive home. My estimate was way off. Instead of being gone for three weeks, we were gone for five. Hopefully Jaclyn hadn't been worried sick.

As we crested the last hill, Prescott spread out before us in the valley below. Home never looked so good.

Jaclyn took up a lot of space in my thoughts while I was gone. I hoped she healed from the loss of our son. It would hurt for a long time, but I was ready to move forward. I hoped she was too. I missed her more than I ever thought I could. More than the Hell Canyon trip. More than Rock Butte.

I smiled when I thought about the unusual start of our relationship. If my parents had not instilled in me a deep sense of duty and honor, I might not be married to her. If Papa hadn't imparted his sage advice, my marriage might not be good or happy.

I remembered the verses I read from Colossians the other day.

Put on then, as God's chosen ones, holy and beloved, compassionate hearts, kindness, humility, meekness, and patience, bearing with one another and, if one has a complaint against another, forgiving each other; as the Lord has forgiven you, so you also must forgive.

When I asked God to show me the way, I thought He did not answer my prayer. But He did. He showed me how to forgive Jaclyn for lying and deceiving me by pretending to be a man. God led me to show kindness to her when she recovered from the fall at Hell Canyon. He gave me the patience to learn to love her. None of those actions came naturally from within me. I was not that good of a person.

And above all these put on love, which binds everything together in perfect harmony.

God showed me the real blessing of putting on love. By choosing to love my wife, I never blamed her for our shotgun wedding. I loved her despite her failures, and she loved me despite mine. In choosing love, our hearts bound in harmony.

After realizing all that, I eagerly wanted to see my wife and tell her how much I loved her. How I prayed we would not lose hope for another child. I knew another child would not take away the pain of our loss, but we could move forward in faith.

A minor part of me wanted to kick Outlaw into a gallop to cover the distance quicker. That was the old me. I learned restraint in the last eight months.

While I was still a few blocks away, I saw Jaclyn and Pearl walking toward the office. Pearl lugged the handcart full of their survey equipment. When Jaclyn looked up and waved, I pushed Outlaw until I was beside her. Then I dismounted and pulled her into my arms in one long fluid motion.

"I missed you," I whispered.

Pearl continued to the office without her.

"I missed you." Jaclyn looked up at me with her one amber and one green eye.

I trailed my fingers along her cheek. "I love you."

She grinned. "I know."

I laughed. "Well, that wasn't what I expected."

"Oh, yeah, I love you too."

Her eyes told me the words were sincere even though her tone teased.

"Well, are you going to kiss your wife?"

"Hmm. Your answer wasn't very convincing."

She pulled my head towards her, and she kissed me. I kissed her back for a minute before releasing her.

"So brash," I teased her. "And on a public street."

"Well, I remember a wedding in a church in Chino Valley gave me permission to kiss my husband."

I laughed deeply. Then I took her hand in mine and walked into the office where the rest of the crew waited.

She spent a few minutes catching up with each crew member. Then she greeted her father with a hug. He studied her for a minute before he smiled. I figured he wondered the same thing I did. Had she recovered from the grief—at least enough to find some happiness again?

"Why don't you take your husband home and get him cleaned up?" Silas asked. "He smells frightful."

Jaclyn laughed. "There's still work to be done."

"We'll see to it," he said. "Go."

We walked hand in hand back to our house.

"Vi stayed with me for a few weeks. She is so funny. There's so much drama as a twelve-year-old. It might sound weird to say it, since she is so much younger, but she was a good friend to me."

"I'm glad. She has such a big heart. Kinda like Mama."

"You're right. I see that is probably where she gets it from."

I held the door open.

Jaclyn walked straight to the stove and started a fire. I pumped water from outside and brought it in to warm in the reservoir.

"How are you?" she asked.

"More in love with you every day."

Her smile made it all the way to her eyes. Not a hint of sorrow.

"What brought that on?"

"Over the last few weeks, there was plenty of time to think. I realized God worked in my heart to show me how to love you like I should as your husband. He showed me how to cherish you. How to live out the vows I spoke to you in that church in Chino Valley."

"You are a good man, Boone."

I retrieved the tub and placed it in the kitchen so I would not have to lug the water so far.

"But I'm not a good man. That's what I'm trying to tell you. I wanted to run. I wanted to be angry. I was afraid to love you. If it wasn't for God changing my heart…"

She poured the hot water in the tub. Then she followed me outside as I pumped more water and took it inside to pour in the tub.

"He worked in my heart too," she said. "It was God who helped me admit my mistakes and to see the pain that my decisions caused. He showed me how to love you."

I stripped down and climbed in the tub.

"So, you don't regret marrying me?" she asked.

"No. Not for a second."

I scrubbed from head to toe, including my hair and beard. Then I toweled off and wrapped it around my waist.

"How are you doing, Jaclyn?"

She looked down at her hands. "Some days I'm still very sad. It hurts less and less as time goes on."

She turned to face me, and she smiled. "I learned that I really want to be a mother."

I wiggled my eyebrows. "Do you, now?"

She nodded.

I picked her up and carried her to our bed as she giggled the whole way.

———

Early in the evening a few weeks later, I picked several full pink roses from a neighbor's garden for my wife. I promised to take Jaclyn out for supper. When I entered the house, I handed her the flowers.

"They are lovely." She took the flowers from me before she placed them in a vase on the table.

Her deep purple silk dress made her skin glow, and my heart thrummed steadily in my chest as I basked in her beauty.

"Not as lovely as you."

"I did not know you owned a suit. And what is that on your head?"

"A bowler hat. All the business owners are wearing them these days."

She squinted as her gaze traveled the length of me. "I don't know. Cowboy hat seems to fit you better."

I grinned as I took off the bowler hat and put on my white cowboy hat.

"Much better."

I held out my arm for her, and she placed her hand in the crook of my arm. We may have gotten everything in our relationship out of order, but I was determined to woo my wife. To give her the courtship she deserved.

"Where are we going?" she asked.

"Do you like steak?"

She giggled. "Of course. I don't think I'm allowed to wear the Colter name and not."

We walked in silence to a new restaurant. Once seated, we ordered. Before our food arrived, I stood and kneeled on one knee in front of her.

"Jaclyn Colter, would you do me the honor of becoming my wife?"

She laughed nervously. "What are you doing? We're already married, silly."

"Shh." I nodded toward another table where her father and my parents sat. "They don't know that."

She laughed again. "They do."

"Go with it, Jack."

"Fine. Yes, Boone Colter. I will be your wife. Still."

"Good. You worried me there for a minute." I stood and pulled her into my arms for a brief kiss. "It would have been really awkward if you said no."

Her cheeks flushed a deep shade of pink. "What's gotten into you?"

"You. You deserved a real, heartfelt proposal." I wanted her to know that I chose her regardless of how our marriage started. She was the only woman for me.

"So, does that mean we're getting married? Again?"

"Do you want it to?"

She smiled. "I'm not sure."

A plan formed in my mind. I knew what I wanted, and I

thought she might like it. It would take a few months for the right time. But I would make it happen.

CHAPTER 35

September 20, 1891

JACLYN

As I rolled out of bed, the nausea hit me, and I ran to find a bucket. I lost the contents of my stomach.

"Jaclyn?" A groggy Boone came into the kitchen as he wiped a hand across his eyes.

I threw up again.

He took a different bucket outside and brought in some water. Then he poured me a glass. "Here."

I took a sip, but my stomach churned, and I threw up again.

He placed a hand on my forehead. "You don't feel warm."

"I'll be fine. Just give me a minute."

"Do you want to stay home from church?"

"No. I still want to go to the ranch for supper. I've been looking…"

I threw up again.

"Maybe a piece of toast?" I asked.

He sliced off some bread that I baked the day before. Then he warmed it over the stove as I sat down at the table. I sipped some water and nibbled the toast.

"Should I make my breakfast?" he asked.

I nodded.

As he fried some bacon, the smell made me feel queasy again. I went into the bedroom and took a deep breath. The feeling subsided as I dressed for church. Then I pinched my nose as I entered the main room.

"I'll wait for you outside." Thankfully, the temperature was mild. Within a few minutes, Boone joined me.

"Sorry, we'll be late."

"It's fine. Are you sure you want to go?" A frown crinkled his forehead.

"I feel alright now."

As we walked to church, I felt better with each step. The last song started as we entered, and Boone shuffled me into a pew in the back next to James. I could not recall ever seeing James at church before.

He smiled at us. "Little late this morning, Boone."

Boone narrowed his eyes and opened the hymnal.

The message lifted my spirits. When we rose to sing the last song, James stood and left. I wondered if he always did that. It explained why I never saw him.

After the service concluded, Boone retrieved our horses, and we followed the family out to the ranch.

"Are you sure you feel alright?" he asked as he rode next to me.

"I'm fine. Stop worrying."

Once we arrived at the ranch, Grady and Deacon offered to take care of our horses. I thanked them and we walked into the house.

"Jaclyn!" Vi ran forward and hugged me. "You look different. All glowy or something."

Hannah looked up from cooking. She studied me for a minute before she smiled knowingly. Ellie Mae remarked on my appearance as well.

"You were late to church, son," Will said to Boone.

"That was my fault. Morning sickness," I blurted out before I realized that was probably not the best way to announce that I was with child.

"What? Morning sickness?" Boone asked me as he gazed into my eyes. "What are you saying?"

"We're going to have a baby." I smiled.

He squeezed me tight. "That's wonderful!"

Everyone congratulated us as we sat down for supper.

"When?" Boone asked after Will said grace.

"I think March sometime."

I saw him calculate backwards and figured he remembered our date in June. The one where he proposed to me. He grinned.

James rolled his eyes and shook his head.

"You should be happy for them," Sam scolded his older brother.

I took a deep breath and let it out slowly. At least Sam came to our defense. Maybe he wasn't angry with us anymore for the survey we did on the corner of his land.

"I am happy for them." James smiled at me. "Truly."

"Thank you, James," I said.

Sam continued to scowl at James, and I was glad they sat far apart during the meal.

"We'll start getting things together for you," Hannah said. "I've been working on a baby blanket, just in case."

I laughed and wished that Papa was there. He sent Boone home early from their survey expedition from Iron Springs to Congress while he finished up with Dustin, Holt, and Allan. I knew he would be pleased to hear the news when he returned.

After supper, Boone helped his mother and Vi with the dishes and told me to sit in the parlor. James left to return to town. Something about not wanting to wear out his welcome. I hoped he and Sam would mend their fences, but it seemed like it would take more time.

I wondered about the conspiratorial glances coming from Vi and Hannah as they talked with Boone. When Ellie Mae told us about her latest novel, I forgot all about it.

Around three o'clock, I yawned, so Boone decided we should leave.

Once we got home, he told me I should take a nap. Since I was so tired, I agreed. I fell asleep praying that God would protect our baby and let him or her make it safely into the world.

CHAPTER 36

November 26, 1891

BOONE

For Thanksgiving Day, I rented a carriage. No way I was letting Jaclyn ride out to the ranch on the back of a horse since she was almost six months pregnant. She often felt achy and tired. I thought about canceling my plans for the day and staying home, but she would not have it.

Silas joined us on his horse, and we rode out to the ranch together. As planned, he distracted her from seeing the decorations in the yard near the lake until we were far enough down the drive that she could not see them.

It was our one-year anniversary. A year prior, we hastily said our vows before God and a pastor who I was certain thought I hurt her because of the many cuts on her face. My plan was to replace those memories with better ones, memories she would look back on and know that I chose her because I wanted her to be my wife, not because I saved her from shame.

I pulled the carriage to a stop in front of the house. Then

I rounded to the other side and helped her down.

"Ugh." She groaned.

A tiny fear tried to take root in my heart as I often worried that we might lose that child too. I pushed it away. She was further along this time. God would protect her and the baby. I hoped.

"Come on inside, Jaclyn," Mama rushed outside to lead her up the porch stairs.

"Where is everyone?" I heard her ask as Mama guided her into the house.

Grady took the horses and carriage to the barn for me.

I brushed the dirt off my suit. Silas slapped me on the shoulder.

"It's time." He winked at me.

Then I walked over to the lake and stood next to the pastor. Our pastor.

I looked over the crowd seated in front of the lake. All my brothers, even a semi-sober Preston, sat there. Our crew waited patiently with their families. They cleaned up nicely. Our friends from church. Even some of Silas's old crew came into town for the event. I smiled as my plan became reality.

Then Silas walked his daughter toward me.

"What is going on?" I heard her ask him.

"You're getting married."

Mama handed her a bouquet to carry, then she scurried around to take her seat next to Papa. Jaclyn scanned the crowd and smiled. Then her gaze found mine across the distance. She looked radiant as Silas led her up the aisle. When she was at the front, she placed her arm on mine.

"You are sneaky."

I grinned. "Shh. Don't ruin our wedding day anniversary."

She laughed. "Alright."

Then we said our vows as part of a traditional wedding ceremony as our friends and family watched. Before the pastor introduced us husband and wife, I asked to say a few additional words to her.

"Jaclyn, I know we made these promises a year ago, and I never once regretted making them. But I wanted you to know today, on your wedding day, that I choose you. No matter how we arrived at this moment, I choose you and only you from now until death do us part."

Her eyes misted. "I choose you, too, Boone Colter. With all your flaws, you are still the only man for me."

I laughed. "All my flaws?"

"Shh. You'll ruin our wedding day anniversary." She winked at me.

The pastor told me I could kiss my wife, so I did. I made a big show of it as I dipped her back and planted a big sloppy kiss on those beautiful lips. Then I raised her fully upright and grinned as I stared into her beautifully mismatched eyes.

Our friends and family cheered.

"Way to go, Jack!" Holt hollered.

I laughed, deeply from my belly, full of love for my wife, both joyous and grateful that she was the woman God chose for me.

EPILOGUE

March 10, 1892

JACLYN

I woke up in the middle of the night, sore and restless. My baby kicked like he was riding a bucking bronco which convinced me he would be a boy just like his wild father.

"Ugh."

"Jaclyn?"

Boone lit a lamp.

"Go back to sleep."

A sudden pain squeezed my insides, and I placed a hand on the wall and stopped pacing for a moment. When I caught my breath again, I smiled at him.

"I'm fine."

He stood and walked next to me.

"Put some pants on."

"I thought you were fine."

"I am, but it just feels wrong for you to walk me around the room in your birthday suit."

He laughed. "Alright."

Boone put on a pair of trousers. "Happy?"

"Ooof." I expelled air quickly as another pain hit me.

He frowned. "Are you having the baby?"

"I don't know. It's my first time."

We paced back and forth for a half hour until the pains subsided. Then I laid down in bed and closed my eyes.

Just before dawn, the pains came again. Then my water broke.

"Boone. It's happening."

He snored at me.

I frowned and smacked him with a pillow. "Boone!"

"What?" he groaned.

"Baby. Is. Coming."

He leaped from the bed. "I'll be right back."

"Boone!"

He turned around.

"Pants?"

His face turned red as he pulled on his trousers again and donned an undershirt.

I groaned as the next pain hit. He returned in a few minutes with the doctor.

"How far apart are the pains?" the doctor asked.

"A few min—" I didn't finish the word.

The doctor instructed Boone to boil some water and gather some clean towels. He stood there frozen.

"Boone!" I hollered at him. "Go."

He hurried from the room.

I wished for a quick delivery. Unfortunately, our baby waited until evening to join the world. Hannah arrived midafternoon after Boone sent word. She helped me while the doctor went on another more urgent call.

"You're doing good," she encouraged me. "Just a few

more strong pushes."

I screamed and pushed. Then it was over. He was there.

I didn't know how much time passed but he cried and then Hannah placed him in my arms. Boone joined me on the bed while Hannah cleaned up in the other room.

"He has so much hair," I said.

Boone held out a finger, and our boy grabbed it. He laughed, and the baby cooed.

"Jaxson," Boone whispered the name we picked out. "Say hello to your mama. Doesn't she look beautiful?"

I snorted. "I doubt that very much."

When Hannah returned, she suggested I try nursing, so I did. Jaxson quickly latched on. A tear slid down my cheek as love for my little boy overwhelmed me.

Once he was satisfied, Hannah burped him and carried him into the living room. She asked Boone to help me change and to put fresh linens on the bed.

Soon enough, I fell asleep.

When I woke next, Boone held his son. "I think he's hungry again."

The image of Boone holding his redheaded son in his arms seared into my memory. The look of awe on my husband's face was something I never wanted to forget. I imagined it matched my own.

Then I took my son in my arms and fed him. I thought back to the day I left California and laughed.

"What's so funny?" Boone asked.

"Just remembering the reason I left Sacramento. I tried to run away from being a wife and mother. To think, what joy I would have missed if I had my way."

Boone sat next to me and brushed my hair back from my forehead. "Good thing the good Lord knew you better than you knew yourself."

I agreed. "Yes, He graciously made our paths cross."

"I am so glad I married you. Twice," he said. "And now, well, I look forward to giving Jaxson some brothers."

"And sisters?"

"Hmm. I'm not sure. If they are anything like their mama, they'll be a handful."

I laughed. "This one is going to take after you. So, I'll be prepared for a daughter like me."

"Yeah, but I'm not sure I will be."

"Boone?"

"Hmm."

"I love you."

He smiled. "I love you, Jaclyn. More and more each day."

I sighed as Jaxson finished his meal. I was grateful for my husband and his family. And my son. The son I never knew that I always wanted.

AUTHOR'S NOTE

Boone Colter is one of those characters that surprised me. I know it sounds strange, since he is an invention of my imagination. His story started with a few brief sentences in *Joy for Mourning (Desert Manna Book 2)* when he ran around wild as a boy before church. That set my mind wondering what kind of a man the wild, rambunctious boy might become. I also wanted to tie his career into the story of the railroads in Arizona. What a better career for the roaming adventurer than the dangerous, multifaceted job of a surveyor.

Surveyors were critical to the westward expansion of the United States. These brave men survived in surmountable odds at times. Their jobs were as dangerous as I described in this book. The most successful surveyors were experts in a variety of disciplines: math, geometry, hiking, hunting, fishing, botany, mineralogy, geology, and more. I hope you enjoyed this peek into the work of a surveyor.

Like most of my books, I diligently researched what life was like for the careers I chose for my characters. I was very fortunate to find some articles online by a surveyor who described how surveying was conducted in the 1800s. I also found pictures and user manuals for the 1874 Gurley Transit that I described in the book. I tried to make Boone and

Jaclyn's job as realistic as possible.

The routes that they surveyed were the actual surveys conducted for the Santa Fe, Prescott, & Phoenix Railway. Some of the sections of the route required multiple surveys, like the Rock Butte section. There were at least four surveys done of that section alone. Hell Canyon was surveyed early on and ruled out as a viable route until approximately 1909, when they decided to build a bridge.

One of the things that I like to do with characters and plot lines is explore situations different from most of the books that I read in this genre. I like to take characters and put them in situations where they are tested and must confront things about themselves. With Boone, I wondered what he would do if faced with an extreme situation where he could choose a sacrificial, honorable path or take the easy way out. I love that he held true to his commitment regardless of what prompted him to first make it.

As a married woman celebrating 22 years with my husband in 2022, I cannot emphasize enough the importance of commitment. Commitment and faith are what helps us persevere in difficult times. The result? A deeper love and commitment than what we experienced before. This was something I wanted to illustrate in Boone and Jaclyn's relationship.

Anyway, I hope you enjoyed Boone and Jaclyn's story. Continue the story with James Colter, in *The Railroad Magnate (Colter Sons Book 3)*.

Karen Baney

Want More Arizona Territory Romance?

Get a FREE novella featuring characters connected to the Colter Sons series! Plus exclusive updates on new releases, special offers, and historical insights from the frontier.

Subscribe at: books.karenbaney.com/larson-christmas

ABOUT THE AUTHOR

Karen Baney is passionate about writing stories full of flawed characters. She enjoys weaving together stories of second chances, redemption, and overcoming personal trials. As a transplant to Arizona, she loves researching the state's history and finding ways to seamlessly incorporate real history and real settings into her novels. In addition to writing and speaking, Karen works as a Software Development Manager for a Christian ministry.

Her faith plays an important role both in her life and in her writing. Karen and her husband, Jim, make their home in Gilbert, Arizona, with their two dogs, Bella and Daisy. Both Jim and Karen are active at Rock Point Church in Queen Creek, Arizona.

Discover faith-laced stories with characters who feel like lifelong friends.

Visit www.karenbaney.com to discover more historical romance series set in the American West. Follow Karen's writing journey and get behind-the-scenes glimpses of her research adventures on social media.

Facebook:	@AuthorKarenBaney
X:	@karen_baney
Instagram:	@AuthorKarenBaney
BookBub:	Follow Karen Baney for new release alerts

BOOKS BY KAREN BANEY

Historical Western Romance

Prescott Pioneers Series:

Step back in time to the wild, untamed Arizona Territory where survival depends on grit, faith, and the courage to start over. Follow three pioneer families—the Andersons, Colters, and Larsons—as they risk everything for the promise of a new life in a land that demands both strength and hope.

A Dream Unfolding
A Heart Renewed
A Life Restored
A Hope Revealed
Hidden Prospects

Desert Manna Series:

Sometimes the most beautiful love stories bloom in the desert. Set in the growing frontier town of Prescott during the early 1870s, these tender romances follow women rebuilding their lives after heartbreak and the unexpected men who help them discover that second chances at love are worth the risk. Set in Prescott, Arizona between 1871 - 1873.

Beauty for Ashes
Joy for Mourning
Oaks of Justice

Colter Sons Series:

Power, legacy, and forbidden love collide in this sweeping family saga set in the Arizona Territory. The Colter ranch empire has weathered decades of frontier life, but now family secrets and buried betrayals threaten to destroy everything. As five brothers—and one resilient sister—navigate the treacherous waters of love, loss, and redemption, they must decide what's worth fighting for. Set in Prescott and other locations within the Arizona Territory in 1887 - 1906.

The Reluctant Cattleman
The Roaming Adventurer
The Railroad Magnate
The Resourceful Stockman
The Restless Wrangler
The Resilient Bride

Larson Sisters Series

Meet the next generation! These delightful novellas follow the three daughters of Adam and Julia Larson from the *Prescott Pioneers Series* as they navigate love, courtship, and finding their own happily ever afters in territorial Arizona in 1886 – 1894.

In Love at Christmas
In Love with the Rancher
In Love with the Horse Trainer

Contemporary Romance

Vargas Ranch Series:

Love is in the air at the Vargas Guest Ranch & Resort near Wickenburg, Arizona. Meet the Vargas family—five swoon-worthy brothers and their cousins who live by their family motto: "We do not deviate from the Lord's plan."

These rugged cowboys run a successful working ranch and luxury resort while navigating the rollercoaster of finding true love.

Falling for a Fake Cowboy
Falling for a Real Cowboy
Honeymoon with a Real Cowboy
Falling for a Shy Cowboy
Falling for a Bossy Cowboy
Falling for a Smart Cowboy
Falling for a Humbug Cowboy
Falling for a Devoted Cowgirl
Falling for a Pregnant Cowgirl
Falling for a Cowboy's Legacy

Steadfast Love Series:

The *Steadfast Love* series follows a close-knit group of friends as they navigate the beautiful mess of modern life in the Phoenix area—workplace drama, complicated families, and love that shows up when they least expect it. These contemporary romances blend emotional depth with authentic faith, reminding us that even when life unravels, God's love never does.

The Heart I Rescue (prequel)
The Air I Breathe

Will I ever put love before my ambition?

They have everything I want…
…something my money can't buy.

My name is James Colter. Everything I touch turns into gold. I'm a successful entrepreneur with everything I could ever want… Except the one thing my brothers have that I don't: true love.

When I finally meet a woman who captures my interest, she's a decade younger than me. She's ambitious and wants an unconventional career.

Should I follow my heart and propose? Will she choose her career or her parents' approval instead of me?

———

If you love emotionally rich Christian romance with rugged frontier grit…

Janette Oke meets Louis L'Amour. Mary Connealy meets Zane Grey.

The *Colter Sons* series blends heartfelt faith journeys, masculine coming-of-age arcs, and sweeping Arizona history into unforgettable love stories.

DESERT LIFE MEDIA

———

Desert Life Media: *There Is Life in The Desert*

Entertainment-first Christian fiction set in the Southwest, featuring redemption, family, and faith

Publishing clean, wholesome, and uplifting fiction since 2010

———

desertlifemedia.com

www.ingramcontent.com/pod-product-compliance
Lightning Source LLC
Chambersburg PA
CBHW051943220626

47052CB00004B/778